The Amish

Widow's Last Stitch

A WILLOW SPRINGS
AMISH MYSTERY ROMANCE

Book 3

Tracy Fredrychowski

ISBN: 979-8-9919988-2-6 (paperback)

ISBN: 979-8-9919988-1-9 (digital)

Copyright © 2025 by Tracy Fredrychowski

Cover Design by Tracy Lynn Virtual, LLC

All Bible verses are taken from King James Version (KJV)

Published in South Carolina by The Tracer Group, LLC

https://tracyfredrychowski.com

To My Loyal Readers,

You are the heartbeat of my stories, the steady presence through every twist and turn, and the reason I continue to write. Whether it's romance, mystery, or a journey of faith, you follow me down every new path with unwavering enthusiasm.

Your support, encouragement, and kind words lift me up on the hardest writing days. You are more than readers… you're friends, cheerleaders, and a blessing beyond measure.

From the bottom of my heart, thank you for believing in me and my stories.

Many blessings,
Tracy

Contents

A NOTE ABOUT AMISH VOCABULARY

The Amish language is called Pennsylvania Dutch and is usually spoken rather than written. The spelling of commonly used words varies from community to community throughout the United States and Canada. Even as I researched this book, some words' spelling changed within the same Amish community that inspired this story. In one case, spellings were debated between family members. Some of the terms may have different spellings. Still, all came from my interactions with the Amish settlement near where I was raised in northwestern Pennsylvania.

While this book was modeled upon a small community in Lawrence County, this is a work of fiction. The names and characters are products of my imagination. They do not resemble any person, living or dead, or actual events in that community.

PROLOGUE

Tragedy Strikes Willow Springs:
Beloved Yarn Shop Owner Dies Suddenly
by Jonas Butler - The Buggy Crossing

Willow Springs, PA - The peaceful town of Willow Springs was shaken yesterday by the sudden death of one of its most cherished Main Street merchants, Widow Esther Yoder, owner of Simply Yarn. Widow Yoder collapsed while dining with her granddaughter, Lizzie Yoder, during a lunch break at The Restaurant on the Corner. She was 72.

Widow Yoder was a well-loved figure in the community, known for her gentle smile and the warm atmosphere of her yarn shop, which she ran with Lizzie. Simply Yarn had become a cornerstone of Main Street, attracting both Amish and English customers who enjoyed her skillful crochet work and her generous spirit.

As the community mourns the loss of one of their most beloved members, many are left wondering if there is more to this tragedy than meets the eye. Simply Yarn will remain closed as Lizzie grieves and considers her future, but the shadow of suspicion now hangs over what once seemed like a peaceful passing.

A private memorial service will be held by her family and the New Order Amish Church. Bishop Schrock has asked the community to respect the family's privacy during this time of passing.

CHAPTER 1

Lizzie Yoder could hardly grasp the overwhelming sense of loss as she sluggishly opened her eyes, praying it was all just a bad dream. The image of her grandmother's contorted face came to mind, her frail hand reaching across the table, trying to hold onto life one fingertip at a time. Amidst the chaos and the murmur of concerned voices, Lizzie remembered leaning closer, her own trembling hand clutching Esther's. Just before the light in her grandmother's eyes dimmed, Esther's lips moved, her voice barely a whisper. "Tell him... the past holds the answers he's searching for."

The cryptic words hung in the air, leaving Lizzie to wonder who she meant, and what secrets her grandmother had taken with her to the grave.

What was supposed to be a quiet, leisurely lunch at The *Restaurant on the Corner* had turned into Lizzie's greatest fear: living life without the one person who meant the most to her in this world.

The crisp September air seeped through the slightly cracked window of her bedroom, carrying with it the earthy scent of fallen leaves and the faint rustle of a distant breeze. Normally, she loved the changing seasons, the way the leaves painted the landscape in brilliant reds and oranges, but today the vibrant colors felt muted, overshadowed by grief.

Lizzie pulled the quilt tighter around her shoulders, staring at the morning light filtering through the window. She didn't want to remember, but the memory forced its way in, vivid and relentless.

The day before had started so beautifully. The crisp autumn air smelled of fallen leaves and faint wood smoke. The gentle clop of horse hooves and the creak of buggy wheels outside the restaurant added to the seasonal symphony. Inside, the warm chatter of merchants taking a break from their busy day filled the space with a lively hum.

Her *grossmommi*, Esther Yoder, sat by the window, savoring her usual bowl of chicken and dumplings. Esther was a pillar of Willow Springs, a woman whose quiet wisdom and kind words were woven into the fabric of the community. Sitting beside her, Lizzie felt a comforting sense of peace in her grandmother's presence, cherishing every moment.

Esther's crochet bag hung from the back of her chair, a familiar accessory that never left her side. Its rounded edges sagged with the weight of yarn and the unfinished Afghan she had been working on. Lizzie glanced at it with a soft smile, thinking how the rhythmic motion of her grandmother's hands crocheting had always soothed her.

As Lizzie reached for her glass of water, a man brushed past their table, his heavy coat trailing close to Esther's chair. The movement was abrupt, almost clumsy, and his elbow bumped against the crochet bag, sending it tumbling to the floor.

"Oh! I'm so sorry," he muttered, bending down quickly to retrieve the bag. His hands were rough, fumbling as he placed it back on the chair. Lizzie leaned over to thank him but froze as a sharp tang filled her nostrils… a metallic, bitter smell that clung to the air like oil on water.

Esther smiled and whispered, "*Ach*, people are always in such a rush these days."

Lizzie nodded and bent to retrieve her napkin, her eyes glancing at the man again. Her focus drifted back to her grandmother, taking another bite of her soup, a look of contentment softening her features.

"Lizzie, dear, you need to find someone who makes you as happy as the yarn shop does," *Grossmommi* had said, her voice warm but with that firm edge that meant she was serious. "David Hershberger seems like a nice young man."

Lizzie had blushed, fiddling with the edge of her napkin. "*Ach,* I'm too busy with the shop to think about such things."

Her grandmother had smiled knowingly, taking a sip of her tea. Then her expression shifted into a slight frown. "Something tastes a bit off today," she murmured, setting the cup down. Her gaze drifted out the window, her eyes distant and thoughtful.

Lizzie had scarcely noticed. She was about to tease her grandmother about being picky when the gasp came... a sound that would haunt her forever. Her grandmother's face twisted in pain, her hand clutching her chest. Lizzie watched in horror as her grandmother collapsed forward, her face hitting the bowl of chicken and dumplings with a splash that sent broth across the table. When she briefly looked up at Lizzie, she whispered her last words.

"*Grossmommi!*" Lizzie's scream had pierced the air, cutting through the hum of conversation. The restaurant fell silent, the diners froze for a heartbeat, and chaos erupted.

Lizzie had dropped to her knees beside her grandmother,

her hands trembling as she tried to rouse her. "*Grossmommi, please,*" she cried. Around her, the world spun into frantic motion. Strangers rushed to help, their movements blurred.

The crochet bag was tipped over again, spilling its contents onto the floor; balls of yarn were rolling away, and crochet hooks were clattering. The earthy scent of fallen leaves wafted in through the open window, a sharp contrast to the shock and grief suffocating the room. Lizzie clutched her grandmother's hand, feeling its warmth slip away with every passing second... *Grossmommi* was gone.

The whispers started almost immediately. A heart attack or stroke, people speculated... it was *Gott's* will. There was no need for a coroner or an autopsy in their community. But for Lizzie, doubt gnawed at her heart.

Her grandmother had been different in the weeks leading up to this day. Distracted. Secretive. Small amounts of money had gone missing from *Simply Yarn,* and Lizzie had caught her grandmother hurriedly tucking something away more than once. There were pieces scattered, unexplained, that didn't fit together.

Now, in the stark stillness of her bedroom, Lizzie pressed her hands to her face, her tears spilling over. She couldn't shake the sense that something wasn't right. Her grandmother's death wasn't just an unfortunate event. It was a thread in a larger, darker pattern, and Lizzie knew she had to pull at it.

Who would want to harm her *grossmommi*? And more daunting still, how would Lizzie find the courage to face the truth while running *Simply Yarn* on her own?

Lizzie sat on the edge of her bed, the strain of the morning pressing down on her chest like a heavy quilt. She hadn't moved since waking, the memories of her grandmother's final moments replaying endlessly in her mind.

The quiet of the cottage only amplified the ache of loneliness. It was the same quiet she'd experienced ten years earlier, after a house fire that had taken her parents and three of her *bruders*. That silence had been unbearable, but her *grossmommi* had been there to pull her through, to remind her that life, no matter how shattered, was still a gift.

Now, her grandmother was gone too, and the silence felt endless.

Lizzie glanced at the black mourning dress hanging from a hook by her door, its presence both comforting and suffocating. Ruthie Mast, a friend who had delivered it the night before, had dropped it off without saying much, just a gentle squeeze of

Lizzie's shoulder and a murmur, "We're all here for you."

She wasn't sure if she could summon the strength to put it on. Facing the day meant accepting what had happened. Facing the viewing meant seeing her grandmother's body lying still on the wooden board, awaiting her final pine box that the men of the community would craft with care and somberness.

Her gaze drifted to the dresser, where her grandmother's Bible still sat, a silent witness to decades of faith and prayer. Its frayed edges and worn leather cover bore the marks of countless mornings and evenings spent seeking *Gott's* wisdom. The sight of it made Lizzie's chest ache with longing; the Bible had been as much a part of her grandmother as the gentle cadence of her voice or the steady rhythm of her hands at work.

Lizzie rose from the bed and approached the dresser, her hand trembling as she reached out. Her fingers brushed over the soft, weathered leather, but something caught her touch... a slip of paper sticking out between the pages. She paused, her heart beating as she carefully lifted the Bible. The paper slipped free and floated to the floor, landing quietly at her feet.

Frowning, Lizzie bent to pick it up, smoothing the crinkled edges with her thumb. The words, faint and smudged, stopped her cold: "*E must know.*" Her grandmother's distinctive, looping handwriting was unmistakable.

She stared at the note, her thoughts racing. What could it mean? Why had *grossmommi* tucked it into her Bible? The message was too brief and cryptic to offer any real answers to its meaning. Sighing, she returned it to its cherished spot, resting her hand on its worn cover for only another second.

***

The viewing and funeral would be held at Bishop Schrock's home. There was no question about that. Their small cottage behind *Simply Yarn* couldn't possibly hold the community that would come to pay their respects to one of its most cherished members. Lizzie could almost hear the commotion already; women bustling in the kitchen to prepare meals for the family and visitors, the low hum of men discussing their duties.

She was certain the ministers had already chosen the four men to dig the grave and others to craft the pine box. It was how things were done in Willow Springs. Everyone had a role to play in death, just as they did in life. The community would surround her with love and care, a tradition that would extend well into the next year. Meals would appear on her doorstep, visitors would check in on her, and subtle offers of help would be given without her needing to ask. But none of it would fill the void *Grossmommi's* absence left behind.

Lizzie closed her eyes, trying to summon the will to move. She thought of her remaining five older siblings, scattered in nearby towns. They would come for the funeral, of course. But they had their own families, their own lives. It was why she had come to live with *Grossmommi* after the fire; she was the only relative living close, and there had been no other option. Not that she would have chosen differently. Her grandmother's little cottage had become her sanctuary, a place where they had built a life together, one stitch at a time in the cozy walls of *Simply Yarn.*

Now, her absence made the cottage feel hollow, and Lizzie couldn't shake the fear of what would come next.

The black dress loomed, a stark reminder of the day ahead. She reached for it slowly, running her fingers over the fabric. It was simple but beautifully made, as was tradition. She thought of Ruthie again, likely part of the group already preparing the meals for the family. Lizzie pictured her bustling around Bishop Schrock's kitchen, an apron tied snugly over her waist as she chopped vegetables and kneaded dough, her hands moving with practiced efficiency.

Lizzie knew the community would be there for her. They would hold her up when she felt she couldn't stand. But this morning, standing felt impossible.

She drew a shaky breath and rose to her feet; her eyes red-rimmed and swollen. Her grandmother would have scolded her for letting grief overshadow her faith. *"The Lord carries us when we are too weak to carry ourselves,"* she had said more than once, always with a certainty that Lizzie envied.

"I don't feel carried," Lizzie whispered, her voice breaking. "I feel lost."

Still, she reached for the dress, slipping it over her head and smoothing the fabric over her waist. With trembling hands, she tied her prayer covering into place and stood for a moment, staring out the small window overlooking the yard. The leaves had just begun to turn, their edges tinged with red and gold. Her grandmother loved this time of year.

Lizzie swallowed hard, squared her shoulders, and turned toward the door. The day ahead would be long and difficult, but she would face it. Not because she felt ready but because she knew her grandmother would have expected nothing less.

***

Evert Miller propped against the weathered oak at the boundary of the Amish cemetery, his hands buried deep in his jacket pockets. The first hints of morning frost lingered in the grass. His gaze was fixed on the gathering before him, black-clad figures standing in quiet reverence around the open grave of Esther Yoder, a woman who had once been his friend and confidante.

It had been nearly a year since he'd last set foot in Willow Springs. A year spent chasing shadows and whispers, piecing together fragments of his past. Every lead he'd followed, every thread he'd pulled, had eventually circled back here, to the small Amish community he'd once called home.

The frustration of finding nothing concrete had ultimately worn him down, prompting a break. Taking a leave of absence from the construction crew he worked with in Pittsburgh, he had returned to Willow Springs to regroup, unsure of what he'd find, or if he'd even be welcomed.

The answer to the latter was painfully clear as he lingered at the edge of the cemetery, apart from the gathering. Dressed in his English clothes, he stood out like a sore thumb among the plain black sea. Though no one had said anything directly, the sidelong glances and curt nods from those who noticed him were enough to remind him he wasn't truly part of the fold anymore.

Evert exhaled deliberately, shifting his weight as he scanned the crowd. He wasn't here for the community's approval. He had come to pay his respects to Esther, a woman who had shown him kindness when he'd needed it most. She had understood him in a way few others did, and her passing left a hollow ache he hadn't expected. But he wasn't there to linger. He was waiting for someone... his cousin Isaiah King, and Isaiah's new *fraa*, Ruthie. If anyone could offer him clarity about what happened, they could.

The sound of the ministers' voices drifted over the gathering, low and solemn, carrying the weight of their *g'may*. Evert shifted his gaze to the simple pine coffin resting beside the grave. Four men he recognized from childhood would soon lower it into the earth, a reminder of the Amish way: humble, unadorned, yet deeply rooted in community.

Evert clenched as he caught a few glances from the men standing near the grave. He wasn't naïve enough to think his presence would go unnoticed. He doubted many had forgiven him for leaving the community or for returning in clothes that marked him as different. But forgiveness wasn't why he was here. Closure was.

As the final hymn began, Evert straightened, his attention snapping to Isaiah and Ruthie who had whispered something between them, and Isaiah gave a small nod, his expression serious yet calm.

Evert lingered a moment longer before pushing off the tree. He kept his movements slow, deliberate, not wanting to draw attention. He had no desire to disrupt the somber moment; he only wanted a few minutes with Isaiah before the crowd dispersed.

As the hymn ended and the gathered community began to murmur among themselves, Evert slipped along the fringe of the cemetery, his boots crunching against the gravel path. His eyes darted to a few familiar faces, noting the way some quickly averted their gaze while others openly stared. It didn't matter. His focus was on Isaiah and Ruthie.

As he approached, Isaiah turned, his sharp blue eyes narrowing somewhat as Evert stopped a few feet away, his hands still tucked into his jacket pockets.

"Isaiah," Evert said, nodding toward his cousin.

Isaiah regarded him for a moment, his expression unreadable, before he stepped forward. "Evert," he said, his voice a deep rumble. "It's been a while."

Evert gave a small, almost sheepish smile. "*Jah*, it has. I didn't mean to interrupt; I just wanted a moment to talk. If you have time."

Isaiah exchanged a glance with Ruthie, who nodded gently before stepping back to give them space. "We'll talk," Isaiah said, his tone firm but not unkind. "Let's walk."

Isaiah stopped near the wooden fence at the edge of the property, his gaze focused on the distant fields. Ruthie lingered a few steps behind, giving the cousins their privacy but staying close enough to be at her husband's side.

Evert shifted uneasily. "I heard about Esther," he began, his voice low. "I'm sorry for Lizzie. For everyone."

Isaiah nodded solemnly. "She was a good woman. Lizzie's going to have a hard time without her."

Evert hesitated, then took a step closer. "I need to know what happened. How did she die?"

Isaiah turned toward him, his expression cautiously neutral. "It's not for us to question. Esther lived a full life. It was *Gott's* will that her time here ended."

Evert's jaw tightened, frustration bubbling beneath the surface. "Come on, Isaiah. You know that doesn't sit right with me. All the paths I've followed this past year kept leading me back here... to Willow Springs. To her. And now, out of nowhere, she's gone?"

Isaiah's eyes locked on Evert's. "She was old, and these things just happen. As far as anyone knows, she died of a heart attack. Instantly. There's nothing more to it."

"Is there?" Evert pressed, his voice rising slightly. "Because I've heard things. Whispers around town. People saying it seems... *suspicious*."

Isaiah's brows knit together. "And what good does repeating those whispers do? Digging into such things is not our way. Lizzie's already hurting enough without someone stirring up more pain."

Evert turned away, pacing a few steps before facing Isaiah again. "I'm not trying to hurt Lizzie. But this isn't just about her. It's about everything I've been chasing. Every clue, every dead end, it all brought me back here. To Esther Yoder. You can't tell me that's just a coincidence."

Isaiah folded his arms across his chest, his stance solid and unyielding. "What I'm telling you is to let it be. Esther is gone, and whatever brought you back here isn't going to change that. Stirring up trouble won't bring her back, and it won't bring you the answers you're looking for."

Evert's shoulders slumped a little, the burden of Isaiah's words sinking in. But the nagging feeling in his gut refused to be silenced. "It doesn't make sense. None of it. I just... I can't let it go."

Isaiah sighed, glancing back toward Ruthie, who gave him an encouraging nod. Turning back to Evert, his voice softened. "If you want answers, you're going to have to be careful. Lizzie doesn't need to worry anymore right now. And neither does the community."

Evert met his cousin's gaze, the determination in his eyes unwavering. "I'll be careful, but I can't promise I'll stop looking for the answers that drew me back here."

Isaiah's lips pressed into a thin line, but he nodded. "Just remember, some answers bring more questions. And not all questions need answering."

CHAPTER 2

The steady pitter-patter of rain against the kitchen window mirrored Lizzie's mood. The gray light filtering through the glass made the small cottage feel colder and lonelier. Lizzie tried to focus on straightening the kitchen, stacking plates, wiping crumbs from the counter, but her mind kept snagging on little things that reminded her of her grandmother's absence.

The cup her grandmother had used that morning still sat on the table, its delicate porcelain now cold and empty. Beside it lay her journal, the worn cover a familiar sight but now a painful reminder of what was lost. Lizzie had left them there deliberately, finding some small comfort in seeing them exactly as they'd been. The arrangement made the space feel as if her grandmother might walk through the door at any moment, ready to settle at the table with her steady hands folding over the journal as she sipped her tea. But Lizzie knew better.

She sighed and reached for the journal, her fingers

hesitating as they brushed the cover. Her chest tightened, a mixture of longing and dread filling her. She willed herself to open it, to see what she had written in those final days, but the pain was still too raw, too fresh.

"I can't," she whispered to herself, shaking her head. Her hand trembled as she picked up the book and carried it into the front room. She knelt by the sideboard and slid the journal into the bottom drawer, tucking it beneath a stack of crochet pattern books. Out of sight, but not out of mind.

A light knock at the door startled her as she rose and returned to the kitchen. The sound was so soft she almost thought she'd imagined it, but it came again, tentative and hesitant.

Lizzie smoothed her apron and crossed to the door, pulling it open to find Ella Stutzman standing on the stoop. The young girl, just twenty, clutched a small basket wrapped in a towel. Her cheeks were flushed as she ducked under the porch's awning, trying to keep the rain at bay.

"Ella," Lizzie said, surprised. She stepped aside, motioning for the girl to come inside. "You're soaked."

Ella hesitated, her hand tightening on the basket's handle. "I... I didn't want to bother you," she said, her voice soft and shaky. "I just... Esther always told me to bring cookies when someone needed cheering up."

Lizzie blinked, taken aback by the depth of emotion in the girl's voice. Ella stepped inside, her movements cautious, as if afraid to disturb the house. The rain dripping from her shawl made soft patterns on the floor, but Ella didn't seem to notice.

"I should've come sooner," Ella continued, holding out the basket. "I wanted to, but... I couldn't. I couldn't bring myself to step inside without her here. It didn't feel right."

Lizzie took the basket, her throat tightening as she looked at the girl. Her grandmother had a soft spot for Ella from the moment she arrived, encouraging Lizzie to befriend the young girl. But Lizzie, nearly eight years older, had never seen the point. Ella was so quiet and cautious, and Lizzie had her circle of friends. She'd assumed they had nothing in common.

Now, standing in the kitchen, the rain-soaked girl looked so lost that Lizzie's heart softened. "You didn't have to come at all, but I'm glad you did."

Ella nodded; her eyes fixed on the floor. "She was... she was always so kind to me," she said. "I just wanted to say, I'm sorry."

Lizzie set the basket on the table and stepped closer, placing a hand on Ella's arm. "You don't have to apologize. *Grossmommi* cared about you. I know she'd be happy you came."

Ella's lip quivered, and she quickly wiped her eyes with the back of her hand. "If you need anything," she said, her voice trembling, "I'm just next door. Uncle Jacob said I should offer to help. He even said he could free up some time in the herb shop so I could lend a hand in the yarn shop if you needed it. But I don't want to intrude."

Lizzie studied the girl momentarily, feeling the same sense of unease she always felt around her. Ella was polite, even kind, but there was a distance about her, a way she seemed to linger on the edges of every interaction, never fully stepping into the circle. Though she wore Amish clothes and spoke Pennsylvania Dutch fluently, there was something... different. Something Lizzie couldn't quite put her finger on.

Ella had only come to live with her Uncle Jacob six months ago, leaving a community in the Midwest. Lizzie didn't know much about the Amish settlements in Wisconsin, and perhaps that was why Ella seemed so standoffish; it was simply a difference in upbringing. Yet the way Ella avoided eye contact or spoke so carefully, as if weighing every word, made Lizzie wonder. Had *Grossmommi* noticed it too? And if she had, what had she made of it?

"You're not intruding," Lizzie said. She hesitated, then added, "I may have to take you up on your offer to help at *Simply Yarn*. I'm not sure when I'll open back up, but it will be soon."

Ella looked up, her eyes wide with surprise. "I'd like that," she said delicately.

For a moment, the silence between them was broken only by the rain. Then Ella gave a small nod and turned toward the door. "I'll let you get back to your day."

Lizzie watched as the young girl disappeared into the misty gray rain, her small figure swallowed by the weather. As Lizzie closed the door, her eyes drifted back to the table where the teacup still sat, and the quiet kindness she still had to give.

***

The early morning sun shone through the windows of *Simply Yarn,* adding streaks across the hardwood floors. Lizzie moved through the shop, straightening skeins of yarn on the shelves and dusting the counter. The shop had been closed for a week since her grandmother's passing, but today she decided it was time to open the doors again.

It wasn't just about resuming business; it was about finding a sense of purpose, of normalcy, in a world that now felt fractured.

She walked to the front door, flipped the sign to *Open,* and propped it ajar to let the warm rays of sunlight spill in. The light, coupled with the soft sound of birds chirping outside, brought a small measure of peace. Lizzie inhaled profoundly, the familiar scents of the shop: wool, lavender sachets, and the faint tang of autumn grounded her in the moment.

The list of tasks loomed ahead: unpacking a shipment of specialty yarns, reconciling the ledger, and catching up on orders promised to regular customers. But as she bent to sort the skeins in a recently delivered box, someone cleared their throat and made her look up.

There he was... *Evert Miller.*

He stood in the doorway, framed by the morning light, his broad shoulders filling the space. His dark hair was damp from an early morning shower and his intense, questioning eyes fixed on her. The sight of him sent a ripple of unease through Lizzie, though she wasn't sure why. Perhaps it was because she hadn't expected to see him, or perhaps it was because his presence always seemed to carry an air of mystery that unsettled her.

Lizzie straightened, brushing her hands on her apron. "Evert," she said, keeping her tone neutral. "What brings you here?"

He stepped inside. His movements were deliberate, unhurried, as though he knew his presence demanded attention. "I thought I'd check in," his voice carried a quiet intensity. "See how you're holding up."

Lizzie's brow furrowed slightly. It was an odd gesture coming from him, a man whose reputation for trouble had preceded him for as long as she could remember. Growing up, she'd only known him as the rebellious boy who couldn't follow the rules, the one whose name always came up when something went wrong. He had left the community years ago, and for a while, it seemed like he had vanished entirely.

But then he'd returned last year, staying only long enough to remind everyone of why they hadn't forgotten him. There were stories of arguments with the bishop, of nights spent in town instead of under an Amish roof. Evert had always seemed to walk the line between belonging and rejecting everything their *g'may* stood for. And yet, for some reason, her grandmother had thought the world of him.

Lizzie folded her arms across her chest, studying him. "I didn't expect to see you in Willow Springs again," she admitted.

He gave a small, almost sheepish smile, though there was no mistaking the intensity in his eyes. "I didn't expect to be back. But here I am."

Lizzie hesitated, unsure of what to say. Evert had always been a mystery, a blend of charm and rebellion that left people either drawn to him or wary. She wasn't sure where she stood, but her grandmother's faith in him lingered in her mind.

"I heard about Esther." After a moment, his voice softened. "I'm sorry. She was... one of a kind."

Lizzie swallowed hard, nodding. "She was."

He shifted his weight, running a hand through his damp hair. "I don't mean to intrude, but I need to ask you something. It's important."

Lizzie's stomach tightened. "*Jah?*"

Evert glanced toward the counter, then back at her. "Did she ever mention the names Nathan or Rebecca to you?"

Lizzie's brows knit together as she tried to process Evert's question. "Nathan and Rebecca?" she repeated, shaking her head. "No, I don't think I've ever heard her mention those names. Who are they?"

Evert exhaled sharply, his jaw tightening as he glanced toward the window, his eyes darkening with frustration. "They're my biological parents," he admitted, his voice quieter now, almost hesitant. "I've been searching all year, trying to piece together who they were. Every lead I've followed keeps circling back to Willow Springs... and to Esther."

Lizzie felt a twinge of sympathy at the vulnerability in his voice. She set aside the skein of yarn in her hands and stepped closer. "Why do you think she knew something?"

Evert met her gaze, the intensity in his eyes tempered by a flicker of sadness. "I talked to her the day before she died," he said, his voice steady but tinged with emotion. "It wasn't a long visit. She said she was busy getting ready for the day and would talk to me later about what she knew."

Lizzie's chest tightened at the thought of her grandmother keeping such a secret. "Did she tell you anything?"

"She said she might have information, but she didn't explain," Evert replied, his hands balling into fists at his sides. "She said it was complicated and that she'd tell me more the next time we talked." His voice cracked a tad, and he looked away, blinking rapidly. "But there wasn't a next time, was there?"

Lizzie felt her throat tighten. She could see the frustration and pain etched into his face, and for the first time, she saw Evert not as the bad boy with a shadowy reputation but as someone deeply wounded by the unanswered questions of his past.

"I'm sorry," she replied tenderly, her words feeling inadequate. "I wish I could help."

Evert nodded, though the movement was stiff, his frustration simmering just beneath the surface. "I hoped she might have mentioned something to you. Anything. Even a hint?"

Lizzie hesitated, her mind flashing back to the journal she'd tucked away in the sideboard drawer. The memory sent a chill down her spine. "I... I can check her things," she offered cautiously. "She wrote in her journal almost every day. Maybe there's something in there."

Evert's head snapped up, hope flickering in his eyes. "Would you?" he asked, his voice almost desperate. "I'd be grateful."

Lizzie nodded slowly. "I'll look. I can't promise there's

anything, but if I find something, I'll let you know."

"*Denki.*" His words were simple, but the weight behind them was clear. He stepped back, his gaze lingering on her for a moment before he turned toward the door.

Evert nodded again and left the shop, the bell above the door jingling softly in his wake as he pulled it shut. Lizzie stood still for a moment, staring after him. The quiet of the shop settled around her again, but her mind churned with questions, but only until another customer stepped inside, directing her focus to the wall of pink yarn.

***

The soft murmur of customers filled the air as Lizzie moved behind the counter, her hands skillfully organizing a display of pastel yarns. The delicate pinks and whites of the collection reminded her of her grandmother's knack for recommending just the right shades for baby blankets and sweaters.

"Excuse me, dear," an older English woman's voice interrupted her thoughts.

Lizzie looked up to find a familiar face, a customer she recognized from her grandmother's regular clientele. The woman, dressed in a floral blouse and navy slacks, held up two skeins of pink yarn, her brow furrowed in concentration.

"Which of these do you think would be better for a baby sweater?" the woman asked, holding the skeins up for comparison. "I can't decide between the soft blush or the brighter rose."

Lizzie smiled faintly, stepping closer to inspect the options. "The blush is more traditional for a baby sweater," she suggested. "But the rose has a warmth that might stand out nicely."

The woman nodded thoughtfully; her lips pursed. "Esther always had such a knack for this," she said with a wistful sigh, leaning in closer to be sure only Lizzie heard her words. "I was in here a week or so ago, hoping to ask her opinion, but... well, it didn't seem like a good time."

Lizzie's heart skipped a beat at the mention of her grandmother. "Why not?" she asked, her tone careful but curious.

The woman hesitated, glancing down at the yarn in her hands. "She seemed to be having a rather heated discussion with someone in the back room. I didn't want to intrude, so I left and thought I'd come back the next day... but that was the day she...

passed."

Lizzie felt her pulse quicken. "Do you remember anything about the person she was talking to?"

The woman frowned as if trying to recall. "Not much. He was a younger man, I think. He wore a different kind of straw hat than what I see around here. His voice was gruff, and he sounded upset about something."

Lizzie leaned forward a little, her curiosity piqued. "Did you hear what they were arguing about?"

"Not clearly," the woman admitted. "It seemed... serious, though. The tone was sharp, and I got the feeling it was a private matter. That's why I left; I didn't want to make things awkward."

Lizzie nodded, masking her disappointment. "Thank you for telling me."

The woman offered a sympathetic smile, placing the chosen yarn near the register. "Your grandmother was a wonderful woman. It's clear she meant a lot to so many people."

Lizzie rang up the purchase, her mind still turning over the new piece of information and why she didn't see the strange visitor. Then she remembered she had gone to the post office that day, leaving her grandmother in the shop alone. As the woman left, Lizzie stood behind the counter, staring at the skein of yarn the woman had left behind.

The image of her grandmother arguing with a stranger in the back room refused to leave her mind. Whoever he was, and whatever the argument had been about, Lizzie felt certain it wasn't as innocent as it seemed.

***

The cottage was quiet except for the soft ticking of the mantel clock and the occasional creak of the floorboards as Lizzie moved about. The oil lamp on the small wooden table illuminated her grandmother's worn journal. Lizzie sat down, hesitating as her fingers brushed the leather cover.

Taking a deep breath, she opened the journal. The familiar slanted handwriting filled the pages, each word carrying echoes of her grandmother's voice. At first, the entries were what she expected: daily musings about the shop, prayers for the community, and reflections on her life. Lizzie smiled faintly as she read her grandmother's words about the satisfaction of a freshly stocked shelf or the joy of seeing Lizzie smile during their shared work.

But then, as she flipped further, the tone shifted.

Mentions of "E" and "R" began to appear in scattered entries, cryptic and vague. Lizzie frowned, reading one passage aloud under her breath: *"E deserves to know the truth. R's part cannot be ignored."*

Lizzie leaned back in her chair, her brow furrowing. *E...* could that mean Evert? And who was *R... could that be Rebecca?* She flipped to another page, her eyes scanning for more clues. Most of the entries were fragments, incomplete thoughts that left more questions than answers.

On one page, her grandmother had scribbled in the margins: *"Ask Jacob about herbal toxicity."*

Lizzie froze, staring at the words. That was odd. Why would she need to know about something like that?

She turned another page, her breath catching as she read a single line: *"The truth will finally bring closure."*

Lizzie stared at the words, confusion swirling in her mind. What truth? Closure for whom? Her chest tightened as she considered the possibilities. Could this be related to Evert's search for his parents? Or was there something else her grandmother had been hiding, something she had been trying to resolve before her death?

Her hands trembled as she closed the journal. Guilt washed over her for reading such private thoughts, but the cryptic nature of the entries left her no choice. Her grandmother had always been an open book in life, sharing her wisdom freely, yet these entries suggested there was a part of her that had been guarded, even secretive.

Lizzie blew out the oil lamp, the room plunging into darkness except for the faint glow of moonlight through the window. As she climbed into bed, pulling the quilt securely around her, her thoughts drifted back to Evert and the urgency in his voice when he'd asked about Nathan and Rebecca.

Sleep didn't come easily that night. The significance of the journal's words lingered over Lizzie's thoughts as the cottage settled into silence once more.

CHAPTER 3

The cottage felt impossibly small and overwhelmingly full all at once. Lizzie stood in the doorway of the room that had always served as her grandmother's unofficial "collection point." Boxes were stacked nearly to the ceiling, and shelves bowed under the weight of jars, old books, fabric, and yarn that seemed to have no particular purpose. A dusty oil lamp perched precariously on a stack of mismatched baskets, and the faint smell of mothballs hung in the air.

Lizzie sighed, gripping the trash bag as she surveyed the chaos. *Grossmommi* had always had a knack for holding onto things: gifts from neighbors, scraps of things "too good to waste," and random items that might, someday, prove useful. It was a trait Lizzie had never understood, given their Amish upbringing, which emphasized simplicity and the rejection of material excess.

Now, faced with the daunting task of sorting through it all,

Lizzie felt the toll of the chore ahead and the unanswered questions swirling in her mind. Her grandmother's journal hadn't offered the clarity she'd hoped for—only more puzzles. The cryptic mentions of "E" and "R," the note about herbal toxicity, and the ominous line about the truth bringing closure lingered in her thoughts, begging for resolution.

She bent to tie the first trash bag and carried it to the front porch, the morning sun warming her face. Just as she dropped the bag near the steps, the sound of approaching footsteps drew her attention. Looking up, she saw Evert striding toward her, his broad shoulders and dark hair instantly recognizable. His hands were shoved into the pockets of his jeans, and his gaze held its usual intensity as it landed on her.

"Lizzie," he greeted, his voice steady. "I was hoping I'd catch you."

Lizzie stiffened faintly, caught off guard. She wiped her hands on her apron and squared her shoulders. "Evert?"

He nodded toward the trash bag at her feet. "Looks like you've got your hands full. Do you need a hand?"

Lizzie hesitated, her grip tightening on the porch railing. "I don't know if that's a good idea."

"I get it," he said, his tone gentle but insistent. "You don't trust me. But I'm not here to cause trouble. I just… I just thought maybe we might find something. Something your grandmother left behind… something she wanted me to know."

Lizzie's chest tightened. She didn't want to admit how much she'd been wrestling with the same thought. She sighed, motioning toward the open door. "I suppose I could use your help."

Evert's lips twitched into the barest hint of a smile as he stepped past her and into the cottage. His eyes swept the cluttered room, and something softened in his expression. "Hasn't changed much," he murmured.

Lizzie frowned, watching him closely. "What do you mean?"

He turned, meeting her gaze. "I used to spend a lot of time here. My *grossmommi* and yours were best friends, remember?"

Lizzie blinked, startled by the image. She hadn't realized just how intertwined their families had once been. "I didn't know you came here often."

"Every week, it seemed," he replied, stepping into the room filled with her grandmother's treasures. He brushed his hand along the arm of an old, worn rocking chair near the window. "This was her favorite spot. She'd sit here and crochet while they talked for hours."

Lizzie felt a lump rise in her throat at the memory he painted. She could almost see her grandmother sitting there, her hands deftly working a crochet hook, her voice soft as she chatted with her best friend. "I didn't know you remembered all that," she said, her voice no more than a breath.

Evert smiled faintly, picking up a small jar of buttons and mismatched forgotten treasures from a nearby shelf. "This one's mine," he said, holding it up. "Your grandmother let me keep it here. She said I'd lose it if I took it home, and she was probably right."

Lizzie stared at the jar, the faded label on the lid reading *Evert's Finds*. She felt a strange mix of emotions: nostalgia, curiosity, and a flicker of warmth she hadn't expected. "I didn't realize…"

Evert set the jar back down, his expression sobering. "Your grandmother meant a lot to me. She was… different. She never judged me, even when I deserved it."

Lizzie nodded slowly, her guard lowering just a fraction. "She had a way of seeing the good in people."

"Even when they didn't see it in themselves," Evert added.

For a moment, silence filled the room, broken only by the faint creak of the floorboards. Then Lizzie cleared her throat, gesturing toward the clutter. "If you're serious about helping, you can start with that corner. Just... don't throw anything away without asking me first."

Evert nodded, rolling up his sleeves. "Deal."

As they worked side by side, Lizzie couldn't help but notice the ease with which Evert navigated the space. He knew where things belonged, where her grandmother kept spare jars or tucked away old patterns. His familiarity with the cottage felt both comforting and unsettling, a reminder of how much he'd been a part of her grandmother's life without her fully realizing it.

And as the morning passed, Lizzie glanced at him more often, wondering if *Grossmommi* had seen something in Evert that she was only now beginning to glimpse.

***

The kitchen was warm, the air filled with the comforting smell of toasted bread sizzling on the stovetop. Lizzie set two mugs of tea on the small wooden table, glancing over her shoulder at Evert. He stood at the counter, buttering slices of bread with quick, practiced movements. It was strange to see a man in the kitchen lending a hand, and it caught her off guard.

"*Denki,* for helping," Lizzie leaned against the counter. "I'm not used to this. Usually, the men around here don't even set the table, let alone cook."

Evert smirked faintly, flipping one of the sandwiches in the skillet. "I've been living on my own for a while now. You learn pretty fast that if you don't cook, you don't eat. I guess you could say I've gotten used to taking care of myself."

Lizzie tilted her head, studying him. There was something in his tone... an edge of humor masking a deeper truth.

He slid the first sandwich onto a plate and started the next. "I didn't make it easy for my grandparents, though. I made a lot of bad choices back then. Some might say I still do."

Lizzie folded her arms, intrigued despite herself. "You seem to be doing fine now."

"Looks can be deceiving," Evert replied, his lips quirking into a half-smile. "I've had my share of wild days. Some of it I regret, some of it... well, it taught me a few things."

Lizzie wasn't sure how to respond, so she busied herself by clearing a box from the corner of the room. She dragged it closer to the table, the cardboard flaps bent and softened with age. As Evert finished making the last toasted cheese sandwich, she dug into the box, pulling out a stack of crochet patterns and a bundle of yarn wrapped in tissue paper.

Her hands paused as she unwrapped the bundle, revealing ten skeins of a soft, cream-colored yarn. Lizzie ran her fingers over the fibers, her brow furrowing. "This isn't right," she murmured, holding a skein up to the light.

Evert glanced over, setting the plates on the table. "What do you mean?"

Lizzie shook her head, inspecting the yarn more closely. "This is alpaca fiber. Or at least, it's supposed to be. But the texture isn't right. It doesn't have the smooth, silky feel of true alpaca. And this..." She held up a receipt, her tone sharpening. "It's expensive, far more than we'd ever pay for yarn in our shop. And this business is in Erie, some sixty miles away."

Evert leaned on the table, his gaze narrowing. "If it's not real alpaca, why would she buy it?"

"That's what I don't understand." Frustration crept into her voice. "We carry alpaca yarn in the shop, real hand spun skeins from Bricker's. *Grossmommi* always supported their work. Why would she buy this?"

Evert picked up one of the skeins, thoughtfully running his

fingers over it. "You think it's fake?"

Lizzie nodded, setting the bundle down. "I'm sure of it. The fibers are too coarse. It's not what it claims to be."

"Could she have bought it for a reason?" Evert asked, his voice low. "Something she wasn't ready to share?"

Lizzie frowned, her thoughts swirling. "Maybe. But I can't imagine what. *Grossmommi* wasn't one to waste money on something like this, not when she could get better quality from a supplier right here in Lawrence County."

She stared at the yarn, a sense of unease settling over her. "I'm going to take this to Bricker's. If anyone can tell me what's off about it, it's them."

They sat down to eat, the simple, shared meal filling the small kitchen. But even as they ate, Lizzie's mind remained on the yarn, and the nagging question of why her grandmother had bought it in the first place.

***

The evening had grown quiet, save for the soft rustling of leaves outside as a gentle breeze carried the crisp scent of early autumn. Lizzie sat in her grandmother's favorite chair in the front room, a steaming cup of chamomile tea cradled in her hands and a week's worth of mail balanced on her lap.

She let out a small sigh as she began sifting through the pile. Most of the envelopes were from neighbors and members of the community, their heartfelt condolences scrawled across the fronts. Inside, she found sympathy cards, simple notes of prayer, and offers of help if she needed anything.

Then, among the stack, one envelope caught her attention. It was plain and unassuming, but something about it felt different. There was no return address, and the handwriting on the front, though neat and precise, was oddly familiar. The postage marking struck her as odd... Erie, not Willow Springs or anywhere nearby.

Curious, Lizzie set her tea down and tore open the envelope, careful not to damage the contents. Inside was a single sheet of paper, folded neatly. As she unfolded it, her brow furrowed at the sparse message:

Keep the past buried and Evert Miller at arm's length if you know what's good for you.

Lizzie's stomach turned as she read the words again, her hands trembling slightly. The note was unsigned, but its tone was unmistakably threatening.

Turning the envelope over, she examined the postmark again. Why would someone from Erie send her such a letter? And why now? Her heart pounded as her thoughts spiraled. Did this have to do with the cryptic entries in *Grossmommi's* journal? The mention of herbal toxicity? Or the skeins of suspicious yarn?

Lizzie set the letter on the table and leaned back in the chair, trying to steady her breathing. Her gaze drifted to the small pile of condolence cards still in her lap, their warm words now feeling oddly hollow against the sharpness of the warning note.

Whoever had sent this letter wanted her to stop. But stop what? She wasn't even sure what it was about her, the past, and Evert that had someone on edge. Yet the tone of the message made it clear that someone believed her grandmother's affairs were better left untouched.

Her eyes flicked back to the letter. *Grossmommi* had written in her journal that the truth would bring closure. If someone didn't want her to find that truth, then maybe it was even more important for her to keep looking.

Clutching the letter, Lizzie stood and walked to the desk in the corner of the room. She opened a small drawer, sliding the note inside along with the journal and the mysterious yarn receipt. This wasn't something she could ignore, but she would need time and help to unravel the threads of this growing mystery.

As the cottage settled into stillness again, Lizzie picked up her tea and took a sip, her gaze lingering on the shadowed corners of the room. She didn't know who had sent the letter or why, but she knew one thing for certain: Her *Grossmommi's* affairs were far from simple, and the answers wouldn't come easily. Suddenly, she had the uncanny desire to share the note with Evert.

***

The faint scent of wood shavings and oil filled the air in the back of Evert's cousin, Isaiah's, buggy shop, where he'd set up his makeshift living quarters. A cot sat efficiently in the corner, next to a small wooden table piled with papers and a flickering lantern. The hum of crickets outside provided a constant backdrop to the otherwise quiet space.

Evert sat on the edge of his cot, flipping through the same notes he'd gone over countless times. The pieces didn't fit, nothing about his parents' disappearance made sense. He leaned back against the wall, rubbing a hand across his face, the exhaustion of chasing shadows pressing heavily on him.

A sharp knock at the door startled him. He frowned, glancing at the clock. It was well past evening, and Isaiah had already gone home for the night. Rising, he crossed the room and opened the door.

Lizzie stood on the threshold, clutching a journal tightly to her chest. The glow of the lantern illuminated her determined expression, though he could see the nervous energy beneath it.

"Lizzie?" Evert said, surprised. "What are you doing here this late?"

She hesitated for a moment before stepping inside, her gaze sweeping across the modest space. "I needed to talk to you about something I got in the mail today and something I found in *Grossmommi's* journal."

Evert stepped aside, closing the door behind her. "Of course. What is it?"

Lizzie moved toward the small table and placed the journal on top of his scattered notes. "This was her journal. I've been reading through it, trying to make sense of things. At first, it was just her usual thoughts and prayers, but then I found… this." She flipped the journal open to a page she had marked, pointing to a line in the margin: *"Ask Jacob about herbal toxicity."*

Evert leaned over the table, his brow furrowing as he read the words. "Jacob Stutzman?" he asked, looking up at her. "Why would she need to ask him about that?"

Lizzie shook her head, her fingers curling around the perimeter of the journal. "I don't know. *Grossmommi* never wrote things like this. Most of her entries were private thoughts or prayers. This feels... different."

She hesitated, her voice faltering for a moment before she continued. "And... I can't stop thinking about how sudden her death was. She'd just had a physical a few weeks ago. The doctor said she was the picture of health. It doesn't make sense that she would have a heart attack out of nowhere."

Evert studied her closely, his brow furrowing in concern. "You don't think it was a heart attack?"

Lizzie's grip on the journal tightened. "I don't know what to think. *Grossmommi* always said we shouldn't question *Gott's* timing, but... something about it feels wrong. She was fine that morning, and then suddenly, she was gone. It doesn't sit right with me."

Evert nodded deliberately, flipping to another marked page,

where Lizzie had highlighted the cryptic mentions of "E" and "R." He frowned as he scanned the entries: *"E deserves to know the truth. R's part cannot be ignored."*

"Do you think this has to do with me?" he asked, his voice quiet but tense.

Lizzie nodded reluctantly. "I do."

Evert's jaw tightened as he closed the journal, setting it lightly back on the table. "And now she's gone, and whoever she thought could bring closure is still out there."

"There's more," Lizzie said, reaching into her apron pocket. She pulled out an envelope and handed it to him. "I got this in the mail today."

Evert unfolded the note inside, his expression darkening as he read the few terse lines: *"Keep the past buried and Evert Miller at arm's length if you know what's good for you."* His gaze snapped back to Lizzie. "Where did this come from?"

"It's postmarked Erie, but there's no return address."

Evert studied the note again, his frustration mounting. "Someone doesn't want us to find out the truth. That much is clear."

Lizzie crossed her arms. "I think she was trying to tell us something."

The lantern flickered, dancing shadows on the walls as Lizzie stepped back toward the door. "I should get home," she said, her voice quieter now. "But I thought you should see this."

"Thank you for trusting me." His tone was sincere. "We'll start with Jacob and the herbal toxicity. It might be nothing, but it's a lead."

Lizzie gave a faint nod before slipping out into the night. As the door closed behind her, Evert thought about the journal and the ominous note, the impact of the mystery pressing heavier on his shoulders. Whatever truth Esther had left behind, it wasn't going to reveal itself easily.

Tracy Fredrychowski

CHAPTER 4

The late afternoon sunlight landed on the polished counter where Lizzie sat, her brow furrowed in concentration. The shop was quiet now, save for a customer browsing the shelves. A stack of receipts and a ledger lay before her, along with the latest bank statement her grandmother had always meticulously balanced.

Lizzie's pen tapped absently on the edge of the counter as she compared the figures, her mind only half-focused on the task. Earlier that year, her grandmother had added her name to her bank accounts, ensuring Lizzie would have full access when the time came. Lizzie's heart ached at the thought; she hadn't realized at the time that she had been preparing for her departure.

But now, something didn't add up.

After pulling the desk drawer open to find a missing receipt, Lizzie's fingers brushed against something at the bottom. With a frown, she lifted the usual office supplies aside and uncovered a second ledger, its leather cover worn and cracked. She had never seen this book before.

Curiosity prickled at her as she flipped it open. The first few entries were dated nearly thirty years ago. Large cash deposits were recorded at regular intervals for seventeen years, each transaction meticulously logged in her grandmother's neat, deliberate handwriting. But what caught Lizzie's attention was the bold notation at the top of the first page: "E's future."

Her breath caught in the back of her throat as she stared at the words. The handwriting matched the entry she had found earlier in her grandmother's journal. The deposits abruptly stopped twelve years ago, and no activity had been recorded since.

Lizzie scanned the pages, flipping through them with growing unease. There were no notes explaining where the money had come from, but on several pages, in smaller writing, were the words "Justice for E." It felt like a puzzle piece clicking into place, though the full picture remained maddeningly unclear.

"Lizzie?" A cheerful voice startled her from her thoughts. A young woman stood at the counter, holding a bundle of yarn.

"Can I pay for these now?"

Lizzie forced a smile, shutting the ledger and tucking it beneath the counter. "Of course," she said, her voice steady despite the storm of questions swirling in her mind.

The customer chatted amiably as Lizzie rang up the purchase, but her attention was elsewhere. Each interruption only heightened her impatience, her fingers itching to reopen the ledger and make sense of the strange entries. What was "E's future"? And why had *Grossmommi* stopped making deposits into the account all those years ago?

By the time the last customer left, and Lizzie flipped the sign to *Closed*, the evening light had begun to fade. She locked the front door and hurried back to the counter; a faint tremor ran through her fingers as she retrieved the hidden ledger.

Sitting at the worktable behind the counter, Lizzie flipped to the first page again. The deposits had been substantial... more money than she had imagined passing through her grandmother's hands. The account bore her grandmother's name, but a chilling note at the bottom of the ledger caught her eye: "Joint Owner: RM."

Lizzie leaned back in her chair, her mind spinning. The questions multiplied. Why hadn't her grandmother ever mentioned this? And what could this account, and the mysterious sums of money, have to do with her death?

The shop felt unusually quiet now, the soft hum of the oil lamp the only sound. Lizzie traced the bold letters "E's future" with her fingertip, the connection to Evert undeniable. But what did this have to do with him?

Her grandmother's journal had mentioned closure and justice. Lizzie couldn't shake the feeling that these ledgers were part of the same story. The truth felt just out of reach, tantalizing but frustratingly elusive. She glanced at the small clock on the wall, knowing she'd need to head home soon.

But not yet. She needed answers. And she couldn't shake the feeling that *Grossmommi* had left her the keys to unlock them, if only she could figure out how to use them. But at that moment, she didn't feel she should share this latest find with Evert just yet.

***

The faint scent of rain hung in the cool evening air as Evert carried the takeaway pizza box toward Lizzie's cottage. Light flickered through the front window, and he hesitated momentarily before knocking, balancing the box in one hand. It wasn't often that he felt comfortable reaching out to someone in Willow Springs. Most folks saw him as an outsider, if not for leaving the community, then for his years of extended *Rumspringa*.

The door opened, and Lizzie stood there, her hair tucked neatly beneath her *kapp*, though a few loose strands framed her face. Her expression softened when she saw the box. "You brought dinner?" she asked, a small smile tugging at the corners of her lips.

He shrugged, stepping inside. "Figured we'd need something to keep us going if we're tackling that spare room again."

Lizzie led him to the kitchen and retrieved a couple of plates while Evert set the pizza box on the small table. "I'll warn you now," she teased, "I've not been back in there since you were here the last time, and it's still a disaster."

He chuckled, sliding a slice onto his plate. "I've seen plenty of disasters in my time. I think I can handle it."

They ate in companionable silence for a few minutes, the quiet of the cottage settled around them. Evert glanced around, taking in the small, homey touches Lizzie had kept intact despite her grandmother's passing. A simple quilt draped over the back of a chair. The faint scent of lavender lingered in the air. It was a peaceful stark contrast to the chaos that had often defined his life.

After dinner, they moved to the spare room, and Evert couldn't help but let out a low whistle as Lizzie pushed open the door. Boxes and stacks of belongings filled nearly every corner, threatening to spill into the narrow walkway leading to the far wall.

"I warned you," her cheeks tinged with pink.

Evert smirked. "This isn't a disaster... it's a full-blown storm."

Lizzie rolled her eyes, grabbing a box from a nearby stack. "Let's get to it, then."

As they sifted through the items, Evert found himself glancing at Lizzie more than he intended. She was methodical, vigilantly opening each box and inspecting its contents before deciding what to keep or discard. There was a quiet strength about her, an unspoken determination that surprised him.

"I don't think I remember you like this," he said, lifting a dusty stack of old magazines.

Lizzie paused, looking up at him with a raised brow. "Like

what?"

"Focused. Determined." He shrugged. "In school, you were always so... quiet."

She chuckled lightly. "That's because I was trying to avoid drawing attention to myself. You and your friends were the rowdy ones."

Evert's smile faded faintly as he leaned against a full box. "Yeah, about that... I wasn't exactly hanging out with the right crowd back then. Got into a lot of trouble I shouldn't have."

Lizzie stopped sorting and looked at him, curiosity flickering in her eyes. "What kind of trouble?"

He sighed, running a hand through his hair. "The kind that gets you labeled a bad influence. After my grandfather died, and my grandmother got sick, I didn't know how to handle it. I felt like I didn't belong here, so I ran. Thought it'd be easier than facing everything."

Lizzie's expression softened, and she stepped closer, her voice gentle. "That must have been hard."

"It was," he admitted, his voice low. "I didn't even know until last year that my grandparents weren't my real parents. They raised me, but I wasn't theirs. Found that out after my grandmother passed."

She placed a hand on the lid of the box, her gaze steady. "That must have been a shock."

He nodded. "It was. And I've been chasing answers ever since, trying to figure out who my real parents are. Nathan and Rebecca, that's all I've got. No clue where they went or why they left me behind. It's like they vanished into thin air."

Lizzie hesitated, her hands brushing the box. "I wish I could help more. *Grossmommi* must have known something, but..."

"She didn't get the chance to tell me." He glanced back at the boxes, shaking his head. "Maybe there's something here. Something she left behind that connects the dots."

As they continued sorting, Evert's thoughts drifted to Lizzie again. There was something different about her, something he hadn't noticed before. She carried herself with a quiet grace that drew him in, and he found himself watching the way her hands moved as she folded an old quilt or how her lips pressed together when she concentrated. He remembered her as the shy girl in school, always keeping to herself. Now, she seemed so much more.

"Do you ever miss it?" she asked suddenly, breaking the silence.

"Miss what?" he asked, pulling an old wooden box from the

pile.

"Being Amish."

He paused, considering her question. "Sometimes," he admitted. "But I've been living English for almost twelve years now. It feels… easier, I guess. But not better."

Lizzie gave a small nod, her expression thoughtful. "It's not always easy here, either. But it's home."

Evert looked at her, a flicker of admiration in his eyes. "Yeah, I can see that."

As the evening wore on, they didn't find anything particularly revealing in the boxes. But for Evert, the night felt like more than just a search for clues.

***

The next day, Lizzie was busy restocking a shelf when the bell above the door chimed softly. She turned to see Ella step in, her small frame nearly swallowed by the oversized black shawl she wore despite the early autumn warmth. The evening before, she had accepted Lizzie's offer to help in the shop, and today would be Ella's first day.

"*Goot meiya*, Ella," Lizzie greeted with a smile, though she couldn't help noticing how the girl's eyes darted around the shop nervously.

"*Goot meiya*," Ella replied, as she fidgeted with the hem of her shawl.

"Come in, don't be shy," Lizzie encouraged, motioning for Ella to follow her toward the counter. "Let's get you started."

Ella nodded and stepped forward, her movements tentative.

"You'll find your apron hanging by the stockroom door," Lizzie said, breaking the silence. "And we'll start by restocking the shelves with this new shipment."

Ella nodded swiftly and went to retrieve the apron. Lizzie waited until she returned before handing her a box of inventory. "I like to arrange the colors in gradient order," she explained. "Start with the lightest shades and work toward the darker ones."

To Lizzie's surprise, Ella caught on quickly. Though her hands trembled slightly at first, they moved with precision as she arranged the skeins. There was something meticulous about her work, almost as if she found solace in the repetition and order of the task.

"You're a quick learner," Lizzie's tone warmed. "Have you worked in a shop before?"

Ella hesitated, her fingers pausing mid-motion. "Not... exactly," she admitted. "But my uncle Jacob said I should learn all I can about running a business. He thought this would be a good place to start."

Lizzie leaned on the table, studying the girl's downturned face. "What brought you to Willow Springs?"

Ella's hands stilled completely this time, and she avoided Lizzie's gaze. "My *datt* sent me here. He wanted me to learn about herbs from Uncle Jacob. He hopes I can open a shop back home someday."

"Do you want to go back to Wisconsin?" Lizzie asked, sensing the reluctance in Ella's voice.

Ella shook her head hastily, her cheeks flushing. "*Nee*. I... I'd rather stay here. Willow Springs feels... different. Better."

Lizzie frowned, curious but unwilling to press too hard. "Why don't you want to return?" she asked mildly.

Ella hesitated, her lips pressing into a thin line. "It's just... complicated," her voice trembled on the fringe of silence.

Before Lizzie could ask more, the bell above the door chimed again. Lizzie glanced up to see Evert stepping inside, his long shadow hovering before him as the door swung shut behind him.

Lizzie couldn't help but notice the way Ella kept her head down, her gaze flitting nervously when Evert entered the room.

Evert was sorting through the box he had placed on the table, oblivious to Ella's unease. Lizzie watched as Ella's shoulders tensed when he spoke.

"I sorted through this box of papers last night, and unfortunately, nothing was interesting," he explained. "I thought I'd put it back if you don't mind me going to the cottage without you there."

Lizzie retrieved the key from her bag. "Just lock up when you're done. I have a long day, and it will be quite late when I finish at the shop today."

Evert looked around. "Anything I can help you with?"

Lizzie heard Ella let out a slight gasp at his offer.

"Ella and I have things under control, but thanks for the offer."

Evert picked up the box and went through the shop and out the back door toward the cottage.

Ella visibly relaxed once he was gone, her shoulders lowering, and her breathing evening out.

Lizzie decided to shift the conversation. "*Grossmommi* always spoke fondly of you." Lizzie watched Ella closely. "She had a soft spot for you, you know."

Ella looked up, her eyes glistening with unshed tears. "She was so kind to me," she murmured. "Kinder than I deserved."

Lizzie's curiosity deepened, but before she could ask more, Ella straightened and reached for another skein of yarn, her hands resuming their precise movements.

Whatever Ella's reasons for being in Willow Springs, it was clear she was carrying more than just homesickness. Lizzie made a mental note to keep an eye on her, there was something about the girl that didn't quite add up. And while she didn't know the connection between Ella and her grandmother, she couldn't shake the feeling that it was significant.

***

Later that afternoon, Lizzie reached under the counter, and her hand touched her grandmother's crochet bag. She hadn't thought about it since the day her grandmother passed, and now the sight of it brought an ache to her chest. She had carried it back to the shop that day, but in the haze of grief, she had tucked it away and forgotten about it.

Sliding the bag onto the counter, Lizzie took a deep breath

and opened it. Inside was a half-completed crochet project, a lap blanket with a geometric design unlike anything she had ever seen her grandmother work on. Her usual style leaned toward intricate floral or simple repetitive patterns, but this was different. The blanket's design's sharp lines and angular shapes felt almost modern. Lizzie ran her fingers over the yarn, noting the rich texture and vibrant hues.

She made a mental note to look at it more closely back at the cottage. But something about it unsettled her, as though it carried a message she couldn't yet decipher. The familiarity of the handwritten pattern left Lizzie on edge for some reason. The instructions were incomplete, as if they had been copied from another source. The flowery script looked familiar, but she couldn't place its origin. It wasn't her grandmother's writing for sure and certain.

Reaching deeper into the bag, her fingers brushed against a lone skein of yarn at the bottom. She pulled it out and held it up to the light. It was the same type of alpaca yarn she and Evert had found at the cottage: soft, expensive, and slightly odd. Turning it over in her hands, Lizzie frowned. The texture felt somewhat off compared to the other alpaca yarn she'd handled in the past.

"Ella," she called, glancing toward the back of the shop.

Ella appeared in the doorway, her hands dusted with a fine layer of wool fibers. "*Jah?*"

"I need you to finish packaging the remaining orders and make sure everything is ready to go out tomorrow," Lizzie said, setting the skein of yarn back into the bag. "I need to run an errand."

Ella nodded briefly, her movements efficient as she turned toward the task. Lizzie watched her for a moment, noting the girl's quiet diligence. Then, grabbing her grandmother's crochet bag, Lizzie slipped on her shawl and headed out the door.

The familiar rhythm of the buggy horse's hooves filled the air as Lizzie guided her brown-topped buggy along the dirt road toward *Bricker's Alpaca Shop*. The owner was a skilled fiber spinner and one of the few people Lizzie trusted to evaluate the yarn. If anyone could confirm whether it was genuine fiber, it would be her.

As the countryside rolled past, Lizzie's mind wandered back to the geometric blanket. Why had her grandmother been working on something so unusual? And why had she chosen to use such expensive yarn that didn't even come from their shop?

The questions piled up, leaving Lizzie feeling more unsettled than ever. She tightened her grip on the reins, urging the horse onward. Whatever answers Brickers could provide, Lizzie was determined to find them.

CHAPTER 5

The sky was tinged with deep purples and oranges as Lizzie guided her buggy behind *Simply Yarn* to the small cottage she called home. The familiar clip-clop of the horse's hooves on the dirt path usually soothed her, but tonight her thoughts churned restlessly.

Her visit to the alpaca shop had raised more questions than it answered. The owner had confirmed that the yarn Lizzie found in her grandmother's crochet bag wasn't genuine fiber. Instead, it was a poor synthetic blend meant to mimic the texture and appearance of the real thing. Lizzie had stared at the skein in disbelief as the woman explained.

"It's not uncommon," Mrs. Bricker had said, her tone regretful as she ran her experienced fingers over the yarn. "Cheaper manufacturers sometimes pass off synthetic blends as alpaca. It's harder to tell by look alone, but the feel gives it away. And this?" She shook her head. "This isn't the real deal."

Lizzie frowned, the puzzle deepening. "Have you ever seen anything like it?"

The woman nodded, setting the skein down on the table. "*Jah*, Amos Zook carries this brand. I've seen it advertised in his wholesale catalog. And there's another shop up in Erie... *Specialty Yarn and Goods* that carry it. I had a customer bring in a skein from there earlier this year, hoping I could match it. She said it was too far to travel for more."

"Amos Zook?" Lizzie echoed, her pulse quickening. "Are you sure?"

"*Jah.*"

Lizzie's mind raced. Why would her grandmother buy synthetic yarn from Amos Zook, or from anyone outside their usual suppliers? She had always been adamant about supporting Plain businesses, avoiding English suppliers whenever possible.

"If Esther bought this," the woman added smoothly, "she must've had her reasons. Your *grossmommi* was a smart woman. She wouldn't have spent money on poor-quality yarn without a good reason."

Now, as Lizzie stepped into the cozy warmth of her cottage, she felt a wave of relief wash over her. She was grateful Ella had been at the shop to handle the end-of-day tasks. Lizzie hadn't expected her visit to the Brickers' to take so long, and knowing someone else was managing things gave her one less thing to worry about.

She lit the oil lamp above the kitchen table, light spreading across the room. Setting her bag down, she noticed a folded piece of paper tucked skillfully beside an empty cup she'd left there in the morning. It was from Evert.

Lizzie,

I found this in one of the boxes I sorted through earlier. It's an invoice from a shop in Erie... Specialty Yarn and Goods. Two boxes of alpaca yarn were purchased a few months ago. Do you recognize the vendor? I thought it was odd your grandmother would order from an English supplier when she always preferred Plain businesses. Let me know what you think.

- Evert

Lizzie frowned, her pulse quickening as she unfolded the invoice Evert had left alongside the note. The details were clear: two dozen skeins of alpaca yarn purchased from *Specialty Yarn and Goods* in Erie.

"Erie again," Lizzie whispered to herself, a chill running through her despite the warmth of the cottage. Twice the name of that city had surfaced in connection with her grandmother. Was it a coincidence, or was there something deeper tying these threads together?

Lizzie set the note and invoice on the table beside the skein of synthetic yarn, her mind spinning. With Amos Zook now tied to this strange yarn, the mystery deepened. Why would her grandmother buy from him, knowing it was manufactured and not spun by the Plain community? And why was the yarn hidden away in her crochet bag, paired with an unusual geometric pattern?

Her gaze drifted toward the journal still resting on the counter, calling her attention back to the cryptic entries she'd read the night before. There had to be more to uncover, more connections, more answers. But the pieces weren't falling into place just yet.

***

A few days later, Lizzie finished her morning tea and settled her mind on the tasks for the day when a brisk knock at the door interrupted her thoughts. She opened it to find Evert standing there, a box in one hand and a determined expression on his face. Without so much as a greeting, he stepped inside, placed the box on her kitchen table, and held up a folded piece of paper.

"This," he said, his voice tight, "is something I just found."

Lizzie took the paper from his outstretched hand, noting the worn edges and familiar handwriting. It was one of her grandmother's unfinished letters.

Evert leaned back on the counter; arms crossed as Lizzie read aloud. "'To whom it may concern,'" she began, her forehead creased as she continued. "'I will not tolerate your harassment a moment longer. If you or your accomplices continue to pester me, I won't think twice about exposing everything I know about your shady dealings.'" Lizzie paused. "'You may think you're clever, but I know the truth, and I won't be intimidated.'"

Lizzie lowered the letter, her eyes meeting Evert's. "She knew something," the words escaped her lips, quiet as a prayer.

"She knew a lot," Evert replied, his tone dark. "And it's tied to Amos Zook and that shop in Erie. I'm telling you, Lizzie, this isn't a coincidence."

Lizzie set the letter down, her hands trembling. "But why? Why would they be harassing her?" She hesitated before adding, "She must've been trying to protect someone."

Evert nodded. "That's exactly what I think. And I'm done sitting around waiting for answers. I'm going to Erie tomorrow."

Lizzie blinked, startled by his sudden declaration. "What? Just like that?"

"*Jah*, just like that. Something is going on here. Your grandmother knew something, and I need to see this shop for myself, and I think you should come with me."

Lizzie hesitated, glancing at the clock. "I can't just leave the shop. I'm not sure Ella… "

"Ella can handle it," Evert interrupted. "You've told me she's catching on fast, and it's just one day."

She sighed, conflicted. "I don't know, Evert. Ella's still new. She's nervous around customers, and… "

"Exactly," Evert said, cutting her off again. "Why is she so nervous? And it's not just around customers. She's jumpy all the time."

Lizzie frowned. "She's just shy. And she's young."

Evert shook his head, his eyes narrowing. "No, it's more than that. I've been around enough shady people to know when someone has a secret, and Ella? She's definitely hiding something."

Lizzie opened her mouth to protest but stopped herself. Deep down, she couldn't deny that she'd had her own suspicions about Ella. The girl was always evasive when asked about her past, and her unease around Evert was noticeable.

"Even if she is, I still feel bad leaving her in the shop alone for so long."

"She'll be fine. Maybe she just needs to know you trust her, and she's capable of handling things on her own." Evert said, his tone impatient. "Tell her what needs to be done and give her the space to prove herself to you. Besides, the sooner we get to Erie, the sooner we can figure out what your grandmother was dealing with, and how Amos Zook and that shop are tied into all of this."

Lizzie glanced at the letter on the table, her mind racing. Evert was right; this was too important to ignore. But leaving the shop, even for a day, felt like a monumental decision.

"All right." Lizzie's voice was steady despite her nerves. "I'll talk to Ella when she gets in first thing in the morning."

Evert's lips quirked into a small smile. "I was hoping you'd see it my way."

Lizzie rolled her eyes but couldn't help the faint smile that tugged at her lips. "I'll be ready."

Evert nodded, stepping back toward the door. "I'll be back by nine sharp."

As he left, Lizzie stared at the letter again. She was determined to uncover whatever secrets her grandmother had tried to protect no matter where they led... and hopefully, it would lead her to find out the true reason why her grandmother died so unexpectedly.

***

The truck hummed steadily as it cruised along Interstate 79, flanked by a kaleidoscope of autumn hues. The rolling hills on either side of the highway were painted in fiery oranges, deep reds, and golden yellows, the trees standing like a patchwork quilt against the crisp blue sky. The occasional farmhouse dotted the landscape, its whitewashed walls and barns nestled amid fields of haystacks and corn, ready for the harvest. Lizzie had always loved the fall, but today, the beauty outside barely registered.

She sat stiffly in the passenger seat, her hands clasped firmly in her lap. The truck's cab was quiet, except for the engine's low hum and the occasional whoosh of passing cars.

Evert had turned off the radio shortly after they left Willow Springs, seemingly out of respect for her Amish ways. But the silence between them was heavy, and Lizzie felt her nerves buzzing with unspoken thoughts.

Her eyes flicked to Evert, his strong hands steady on the steering wheel. His dark hair curled a little at the ends, and his profile was sharp and focused as he watched the road ahead. He didn't look like the boy she'd known from school anymore. He was a man now, an *Englisher* driving her away from her predictable world into the unknown.

"Why so quiet?" he asked suddenly, his voice breaking the silence. He didn't look at her, but there was a hint of a smile tugging at the corner of his mouth. "You've been sitting there like you're afraid to breathe."

Lizzie stiffened, heat rising in her cheeks. "I'm just thinking," she said, trying to sound composed.

"About what?" he pressed. "Or should I guess? Let me see... I bet you're second-guessing coming with me."

Lizzie hesitated, her fingers tightening on her skirt. "I... well, maybe a little. It's not every day I leave Willow Springs to ride off with someone like you."

Evert chuckled harshly, glancing at her briefly. "Someone

like me, huh? What's that supposed to mean?"

"You know what I mean," her words drifted like a sigh. "If word gets back to Bishop Schrock that I went off with you, there will be talk. And not the good kind."

Evert's smile faded, and he nodded. "Yeah, I figured as much." He tapped the steering wheel with his thumb, the rhythm matching the beat of her heart. "I should've thought about that before asking you to come. The English don't think about things like that, but I know it's different for you. I'm sorry for putting you in a spot like this."

Lizzie turned to look at him, surprised by the sincerity in his tone. "It's not your fault. I agreed to come, didn't I?"

"Still," he said, his voice softer now, "I should've given it more thought. I know the rules you live by, even if I don't follow them anymore. I respect them."

His words hung in the air, and for a moment, the tension between them eased. Lizzie let out a breath she hadn't realized she was holding and glanced out the window. The leaves blurred together as they sped past, and she tried to focus on the beauty of the day instead of the knot of worry in her chest.

"All I care about right now is figuring out what *Grossmommi* was up to. And how you fit into all of this." She turned back to him, her gaze steady. "You said she knew something about your parents. If she did, then I owe it to her to help you find the truth."

Evert's grip on the wheel tightened, and he nodded. "I appreciate that. More than you know."

The rest of the drive was quieter but not as heavy. They passed a farmer's market set up along the roadside, its stalls brimming with pumpkins, gourds, and baskets of apples. A group of children ran through a nearby field, their laughter carried by the wind. It was a scene straight out of a painting, but Lizzie's mind stayed on the path ahead.

As they approached Erie, the trees gave way to more buildings and highways, the countryside leisurely morphing into the bustling energy of a small city. Lizzie felt a pang of unease settle in her chest. She had agreed to come, but the farther they got from Willow Springs, the more foreign everything felt.

***

Evert stopped on the sidewalk, studying the sign and noting the names of the proprietors, *Thomas and Miriam Mast*, listed under the business name. He followed Lizzie as she pushed the door open, stepping hesitantly into *Specialty Yarn and Goods.* Evert followed close behind, scanning the shop with sharp eyes. The place was smaller than he'd imagined, but it was packed with shelves overflowing with colorful skeins of yarn, spools of thread, and precisely stacked pattern books.

Lizzie clutched the skeins of yarn they'd brought, her shoulders tense as she approached the counter. Evert hung back near the entrance, letting his gaze wander over the shop. He wasn't much for yarn, but his instincts told him to stay alert. Something about this place already felt off.

"Hello," Lizzie said, her voice steady but polite. The two shop owners behind the counter looked up, their expressions startled by her dress, she thought.

The woman, a sharp-featured lady with silver-streaked hair pulled into a tight bun, smiled thinly. "Good morning. Can I help you?"

Lizzie set the skeins of yarn on the counter. "I'm hoping you might recognize this yarn. My grandmother started a project with it, and I want to finish it. I believe she bought it from here."

The woman's eyes moved to the yarn before darting to the

man standing beside her. He was tall, with thinning hair and a nervous energy that seemed to radiate from him. Evert noticed how his hands twitched as he shifted his weight from one foot to the other.

"This is... unique," the woman said, her smile tightening. "But I'm afraid we don't carry this yarn anymore. It's too expensive, and our supplier has trouble keeping it in stock."

Evert's brow furrowed. She didn't even touch the yarn, let alone examine it. He crossed his arms, watching her closely.

"My grandmother's name was Esther Yoder," her voice calm but probing. "She lived in Willow Springs. I think she bought this yarn from you."

The woman's smile faltered for a fraction of a second. "Esther Yoder?" she repeated, glancing at the man beside her. "I... I'm not sure I recall the name."

Evert saw the lie as plain as day. The man's jaw tightened, and his eyes darted toward the counter. Lizzie noticed it too, her gaze following his to a pattern book partially hidden beneath a folded flyer. Her breath hitched slightly, but before she could speak, the woman shifted the book, covering it more completely.

"Are you sure?" Lizzie pressed. "The project she was

working on looks similar to one I saw on that pattern you just covered."

The man cleared his throat, his voice gruff as he interrupted. "We don't know anything about that. If your grandmother was here, it must've been a long time ago."

Lizzie opened her mouth to respond, but the bell over the door chimed again. A customer entered, and the woman's demeanor changed immediately. "Excuse me," she said, turning to greet the newcomer with forced cheerfulness.

Evert stepped closer to Lizzie, lowering his voice. "They're lying."

Lizzie looked at him, her brows knitted in confusion. "How do you know?"

"Call it a sixth sense," he said, turning toward the man, who was now deliberately avoiding eye contact. "I've seen plenty of people try to hide things, and these two? They're hiding something big."

Before Lizzie could respond, the man stepped forward abruptly and said, "We're closing up early today," with a curt tone. "You'll have to come back another time if you want to ask more questions."

Evert felt his hackles rise at the dismissal, but he put a

steadying hand on Lizzie's arm and nodded. "Come on," he said, guiding her toward the door. "We'll come back."

Lizzie hesitated, glancing back at the counter. "But... "

"Not now," Evert said firmly, his voice subdued. "Let's go."

Outside, the crisp October air hit him like a balm, cooling the frustration bubbling beneath the surface. He led Lizzie to the truck, unlocking the door before turning to face her.

"They know something," his tone edged with certainty. "That wasn't just awkwardness or bad customer service. They were lying."

Lizzie looked down at the skeins of yarn in her hands. "But why would they lie about something like this? It doesn't make any sense."

Evert shook his head, his jaw tightening. "I don't know. But I told you something wasn't right. And now? I'm surer of it than ever."

As they climbed into the truck, Evert couldn't shake the feeling that this was only the beginning. Whatever secrets the shop owners were hiding, they were tied to Esther, and maybe even to the answers he'd been searching for his entire life.

As he climbed into the truck, his mind churned over the strange encounter. Something about the couple didn't sit right with him... something beyond their shifty behavior and the lies they'd tried to pass off. It nagged at him, just out of reach, until he replayed their words in his mind.

Their accents.

It wasn't obvious, not to someone who hadn't lived in both worlds. But Evert had. He'd spent years trying to bury the sharp cadence of his Amish upbringing, softening the clipped sounds and deliberate phrasing that marked his speech. He thought he'd gotten good at hiding it, but every now and then, a word or phrase would slip out, betraying his past.

And now, he realized he'd heard that same cadence in the older couple. Subtle but unmistakable to someone like him.

"They were once Amish," he muttered under his breath, gripping the steering wheel forcefully.

Lizzie looked over, startled. "What?"

He shook his head, his jaw clenching. "Their accents... they speak a Pennsylvania *Deitsch* dialect."

Lizzie blinked, her brow furrowing. "Are you sure? They didn't look Amish, and they certainly weren't acting like it."

"I'm sure. It's not something you just forget, no matter how hard you try. I've been trying to get rid of it for years, but it's always there, just under the surface. And I heard it in their voices."

Lizzie frowned, turning the skeins of yarn over in her hands. "But if they were Amish... why would they leave? And why would they lie about knowing *Grossmommi*?"

Evert stared out the windshield, his thoughts racing. "I don't know yet," he admitted. "But whatever they're hiding, it's big. And I'm not stopping until I find out what it is."

He turned the key in the ignition, the truck rumbling to life. As they pulled back onto the road, the autumn landscape blurred past them, vibrant and vivid, but Evert's focus was fixed firmly on the questions swirling in his mind.

***

Behind the locked door, Miriam tugged the blind aside just enough to peek out. Her hands trembled as she watched the truck pull away, her pulse pounding in her ears. She turned to Thomas, who was securing the door with deliberate care.

"It's him, isn't it?" Miriam whispered, her voice tinged with unease. "There's no mistaking it."

Thomas's jaw tightened, and he turned to face her with a sneer. "Stop it, Miriam. You can't go getting all emotional now.

We're too close to being free."

Miriam's eyes widened, and she stepped closer to him, her voice dropping to a shaky whisper. "But Thomas, what if... "

"What if nothing," he snapped, cutting her off. "The deal was simple; he stays Amish. We both know that didn't happen. He left, which voided our promises to your parents."

She flinched at his sharp tone but didn't look away. "You don't care about him at all?"

"The only thing I care about now is hiding that account from him," Thomas growled, his eyes narrowing. "That's all that matters, Miriam. Remember our plans... seeing him doesn't change any of that."

Miriam hesitated, clutching the edge of the counter for support. "And what if he finds out the truth?"

Thomas's sneer deepened, his voice a low hiss. "Then we make sure he doesn't."

Miriam's breath caught in her throat, but she nodded silently, letting the blind fall back into place. As the two stood in the dimly lit shop, the shadows seemed to grow heavier, the weight of their secrets pressing in from every corner.

CHAPTER 6

Mid-morning light streamed through the window as Lizzie sat at her grandmother's old roll-top desk. The faint scent of old oak wafted up as she opened the top drawer. Papers lay in neat stacks, but something about the arrangement felt off.

Her fingers traced the side of the drawer, and a faint gap caught her attention. She pushed gently, and the bottom of the drawer shifted, revealing a hidden compartment.

Lizzie's heart raced as she warily pried it open, her fingers trembling. Inside lay a bundle of papers tied with twine, the edges yellowed. She untied the bundle, revealing what looked like handwritten lists and ledgers.

Her eyes scanned the first sheet. At the top of the page, written in her grandmother's unmistakable handwriting, were the words: *Amos Zook's Customers – Overpriced and Fake Merchandise.*

Lizzie frowned, flipping through the pages. The list detailed names of local Amish families alongside items they'd purchased: yarn, herbal remedies, and other supplies. All with suspiciously high prices. Some items were marked with a red asterisk, and in the margins, her grandmother had written notes:

Fake alpaca yarn... check quality.

Herbal remedy mislabeled...harmful ingredients?

Lizzie's stomach churned. Amos Zook was a respected businessman in the town, but this list painted a different picture, a man profiting off the trust of his community.

She turned to the next sheet, her eyes skimming as she read a list of unpaid loans. At the top was Jacob Stutzman's name, with dates spanning several years. The amounts were staggering. At the bottom of the page, written in bold, underlined letters, were the words: *He must be stopped!*

Lizzie leaned back in her chair, the papers trembling in her hands. What had her grandmother been trying to uncover? And why had she hidden these records so prudently?

A knock on the doorframe startled her. Lizzie spun around to see Ella standing there, her hands clasped nervously in front of her apron.

"Ella?" Lizzie asked, setting the papers down.

"I'm sorry to bother you," Ella said, her voice soft and

hesitant. "Amos Zook is at my uncle's shop, and he's on his way over to see you."

Lizzie frowned, her pulse quickening. "I'm busy right now."

Ella shifted uncomfortably, her gaze darting to the floor. "He said it's important. I don't think he'll take no for an answer."

Lizzie stood, her mind racing. The papers in the drawer felt like they were burning a hole in her thoughts, but she couldn't ignore Amos's insistence. She caught the flicker of unease in Ella's eyes and realized the younger woman was just as unsettled as she was.

"Did he say what it was about?" Lizzie asked, grabbing her shawl.

Ella shook her head. "No, but... he seemed angry."

Lizzie sighed, glancing back at the desk. "Fine. I'll see what he wants."

Ella hesitated, wringing her hands. "Are you sure?"

Lizzie gave her a reassuring smile, though her stomach churned with unease. "No, but it's fine. I'll handle it."

As Ella left the cottage, the gravity of her grandmother's hidden papers lingered in her mind.

Lizzie stepped onto the front porch, her heart pounding as she saw Amos striding purposefully up the path. His ample frame and dark expression sent a ripple of unease through her. She crossed her arms, standing firm at the top of the steps. "Amos? What can I do for you?"

He stopped at the base of the porch, his piercing gaze locking onto hers. "We need to talk. I've been hearing things about you asking questions you've got no business asking."

Lizzie's spine straightened. "I have every right to ask about my grandmother's business. If she kept records or made decisions, it's my job to figure them out."

Amos sneered, taking a deliberate step onto the porch. "Your grandmother knew how to keep her affairs private. Maybe you should take a page from her book and bury the past."

Lizzie gasped at his reference to burying the past... almost the same words on the note she had received, but she didn't back down. "Are you trying to threaten me?"

Before he could respond, the rumble of an engine caught both their attention. Amos turned, his smirk faltering as Evert's truck pulled into the driveway, a cloud of dust swirling behind it. Evert climbed out; his expression sharp as he took in the scene.

"What's going on here?" Evert's tone was calm but carried a warning edge.

Amos straightened, his gaze narrowing. "Nothing that concerns you, Miller. This is between me and Lizzie."

Evert strode forward, stepping onto the porch and placing himself squarely between Lizzie and Amos. "It looks like it concerns her, and now it concerns me."

Amos's lips curled into a mocking smile. "You're always poking your nose where it doesn't belong, aren't you? Thought you left Willow Springs behind for good."

Evert's jaw tightened; his stance unyielding. "I came back to find answers, and by the look on Lizzie's face, you're bullying her about something."

Amos's face darkened. "I'm not intimidating anyone. I'm just giving her some advice. She's stirring up things that are better left alone."

Lizzie stepped forward, finding her voice. "What things? Why don't you just say what you mean?"

Amos's cold gaze flicked to her. "Let's just say you should start looking closer to home. Your grandmother wasn't the only one with secrets." His voice dropped lower. "Ask Jacob about his business dealings, or that niece of his. They're not as innocent as they seem."

Lizzie frowned, her stomach twisting. "What does Jacob have to do with this?"

Amos shrugged, the smirk returning to his face. "Maybe nothing. Maybe everything. But if I were you, I'd stop digging before you end up in the same trouble as your grandmother."

Evert's hands clenched into fists, and he stepped forward, his voice ice-cold. "You'd better leave, Amos. Now."

Amos held his ground for a moment, then gave a mocking chuckle. "Suit yourself. Don't say I didn't warn you."

With a final glare, Amos turned and stomped back down the path, his boots crunching on the gravel. The tension lingered in the air long after he disappeared around the bend.

Evert dropped his keys on the table inside the cottage and turned to Lizzie. "What was that about? And what did he mean about Jacob and Ella?"

Lizzie sighed and walked to the front room to pull out the ledger she'd found earlier. "It's this. It's a list of his customers, and notes about fake or overpriced merchandise. Jacob's name is here too, with unpaid loans. And now Amos is hinting that

Ella is involved."

Evert's brow furrowed as he flipped through the pages. "How did your grandmother get hold of these?"

"I'm not sure, but it gives a clear picture of what she was digging into."

"Amos reeks of trouble. If he's pointing fingers at Jacob and Ella, it might be to cover his own tracks. Or there's more going on than we realize."

Lizzie hesitated, then pointed to the list that mentioned Jacob's debts. "I have to believe this has to do with whatever she was trying to expose."

Evert studied the ledger, his expression grim. "If Jacob's tied to Amos, it could explain a lot."

Lizzie nodded. "I can't believe that. Jacob is a respected member of this community, and Ella is young and lost, as far as I can tell. She may be hiding something, but I can't believe it's criminal."

Evert rested against the table, his gaze meeting hers. "We keep digging. If Amos is willing to come to your home and make threats, it means we're getting close to something he doesn't want us to find."

Lizzie followed Evert back outside, the sharp breeze tugging at her sweater as they descended the porch steps. Her mind was swirling with questions, and the wind seemed to mirror her unsettled thoughts. Just as she was about to speak, a piece of paper fluttered by, carried on the breeze. Evert snatched it midair, his sharp reflexes surprising her.

"What's this?" he muttered, holding it up. The edges were singed, and the faint scent of smoke lingered.

Lizzie leaned closer to see the faded text: *Invoice #4738 – Herb Shipment.*

Her stomach tightened. "Where did that come from?"

Evert scanned the yard, pointing to a thin trail of smoke rising from behind *Jacob's Herb Shop* next door. "There. Looks like a burn barrel."

A knot of unease formed in Lizzie's chest as she followed Evert toward the smoke. Rounding the corner of the shop, they found the barrel in question, still emitting a faint trail of smoke. The wind had scattered partially burned papers across the ground, the ashes mingling with dry leaves.

Evert crouched down, sifting through the debris with a stick. "Invoices?" He held up another charred sheet. "Looks like someone's trying to get rid of something."

Lizzie knelt beside him, her breath catching as she read the faint text. "These herbs... I've never heard of them before. What are they?"

Evert scanned the names. "Black root... fever grass... elder bark concentrate. Some of these sound familiar, but others... " He frowned. "I don't know. They don't sound like the kind of herbs you'd find in an ordinary apothecary."

Lizzie's hands trembled as she reached for another fragment. "I remember..." Her voice trailed off, and she pressed a hand to her forehead, a memory suddenly surfacing.

"What is it?" Evert asked, his voice sharp with concern.

Lizzie's brows knit together as she closed her eyes, willing herself to focus. "The restaurant... there was an odd smell."

Lizzie opened her eyes, the details coming back in flashes. Her voice faltered. "I couldn't place it, and still, I don't even know if I remember it clearly."

Evert looked back at the smoldering barrel, the acrid smell of smoke filling his senses. "Do you think the scent had something to do with your grandmother's death?"

Lizzie's voice was firm. "I don't believe in coincidences." Her breath deepened as she clutched a half-burned paper in her hands, and suddenly, the name *fever grass* jumped out at her.

"Fever grass... *Grossmommi* mentioned that in her journal. And something about herbal toxicity."

Evert's eyes darkened. "Toxicity? Do you think...?"

Lizzie's mind reeled as she pieced together the fragments. "What if someone used it to... to harm her?"

Evert placed his hands on his hips. "We need to be sure. This changes everything. If herbs were involved, it's not just about money anymore but something much darker."

Lizzie nodded, despite the chill that ran down her spine. "We have to find out the truth."

"We will.

Lizzie shuddered at the thought. "*Grossmommi* always trusted Jacob. She believed in him."

Evert's voice softened. "Sometimes people hide their true selves."

As they gathered the scattered papers, Evert's sharp eye caught something scrawled in the margin of one invoice. He said, "Look at this," while handing the paper to Lizzie.

She squinted at the faint handwriting. *Special batch. Rush order for AZ.*

Lizzie's pulse quickened. "It's all connected. Amos, Jacob, these herbs."

Evert's gaze was steely. "Then we follow this lead. We find out exactly what these herbs are, and why your grandmother was caught up in all of this."

***

Ella stirred the pot of chili, the savory aroma doing little to calm the storm in her chest. She could feel her uncle Jacob's eyes on her even as he shuffled through the pile of receipts on the table behind her. His frustrated muttering grated against her nerves, each word like a hammer against the fragile glass of her composure.

"Where are they?" Jacob growled, his tone sharper now. The clatter of paper and the scrape of a chair made her flinch. "I know I left that stack of invoices here. Last month's orders. They were right here on the counter. Have you seen them?"

Ella's grip tightened on the spoon, her knuckles whitened. She focused on the pot in front of her, stirring rhythmically to hide the slight tremor in her hands. "*Nee*," she replied, keeping her voice neutral, almost dismissive.

Jacob's chair creaked as he shifted his weight, his frustration simmering just below the surface. "You're sure? I need to account for every last detail."

Ella forced herself to turn a little, catching her uncle's furrowed brow and the shadow of worry etched across his face. His shoulders slumped under an invisible weight she could almost feel pressing down on her. "I don't know where they could've gone."

Jacob exhaled, rubbing a hand over his face. "This whole mess is Amos's doing. I should've known better. Thought I could outsmart him, use his schemes to keep us afloat. Turns out all I did was dig us deeper."

Ella's stomach clenched as she turned back to the stove, her heart pounding. She stirred the pot with more force than necessary, her mind racing with the implications of his words. Amos's schemes. His threats. The shop teetered on the edge of collapse.

Ella swallowed hard. She knew exactly where the invoices were, or at least what was left of them. The memory of the burning barrel and the half-charred papers sent a chill down her spine. But she couldn't tell Jacob that. All she wanted to do was hide all traces of her uncle's connection to Amos Zook.

"You've been a good help to me, Ella. Better than I deserve."

She forced a smile, her stomach twisting. She couldn't let him see her fear. Not now, when everything was on the line. "It's nothing," she said lightly, turning back to the stove. "You took me in when I had nowhere else to go. It's the least I can do."

Jacob didn't respond, his silence heavier than his words. As she set the table, her mind raced. Amos was squeezing them dry, and Jacob was right to be afraid. If the shop failed, she would have no choice but to return to Wisconsin, a thought that made her stomach churn. She couldn't go back, not after everything that had happened.

As they sat down to eat, Jacob muttered something under his breath about debts and mistakes, his spoon clinking against his bowl. Ella barely touched her food, her mind too preoccupied with the weight of her secrets and the growing sense that the walls were closing in.

She glanced at her uncle, his face lined with worry, and felt a pang of guilt. He had taken her in, given her a chance to start over. But at what cost?

Tracy Fredrychowski

CHAPTER 7

D rizzle fell in a fine mist, dampening Lizzie's *kapp* and apron as she approached the front door of *Simply Yarn*. The gray sky mirrored her mood, the pressure of the previous day still pressing heavily on her shoulders. She fumbled with the keys, her hands cold and stiff from the morning chill, and glanced up to take in the shop's window.

Her breath caught in her throat.

Across the front glass, in thick, dripping black paint, were the words: STOP DIGGING.

Lizzie froze, her heart pounding as the bold letters mocked her. The paint streaked downward, smearing in uneven rivulets from the rain, giving the words a sinister, almost bleeding effect. For a moment, she stood there, unsure whether to scream or cry. Instead, she did neither, taking a shaky breath and looking around.

The street was quiet, except for the soft patter of rain on the sidewalk. No one lingered near the shop. Whoever had done this had already vanished.

Lizzie's pulse raced as she turned the key and opened the door, stepping inside. She leaned against the doorframe, her chest tight. The message wasn't just a warning… it was a threat.

Before she could collect her thoughts, the sound of tires on wet pavement drew her attention. A black sedan pulled up to the curb, and a man in dark slacks climbed out of it. He adjusted his wide-brimmed hat and walked toward the shop, his movements deliberate and composed. Lizzie immediately recognized him: Detective Powers.

As he approached, Lizzie squared her shoulders, forcing a calm expression onto her face. She had no intention of dragging the authorities into her business. The Amish preferred to handle things within their own community, and she wasn't about to change that.

"Miss Yoder?" Detective Powers called, his voice steady as he tipped his hat.

Lizzie stepped halfway outside. "Detective Powers. I wasn't expecting you."

"I received a call this morning about vandalism at your shop," he said, his eyes drifting to the window and the ominous words scrawled across it. "Looks like someone wanted to send you a message about something."

Lizzie glanced back at the window and forced a thin smile. "It's probably just a prank. Nothing to worry about."

Powers raised an eyebrow, unconvinced. "A prank? This doesn't look like harmless mischief to me." He pulled a small notepad from his pocket and began jotting something down. "Do you have any idea who might've done this or why?"

Lizzie hesitated, her mind racing. She didn't want to mention Evert or the discoveries they'd made. The last thing she needed was more attention on the situation or on Amos Zook. "No, I don't," she said carefully. "We haven't had any trouble before."

Powers gave her a long look, his eyes narrowing faintly. "I find it hard to believe this is about competition. Do you have any reason to believe someone might want to intimidate you?"

Lizzie shook her head. "We're a small community. People get along, for the most part."

Powers sighed, tucking his notepad away. "I can understand wanting to handle things within your community, Miss Yoder, but threats like this shouldn't be taken lightly. If you remember anything, anything at all, you need to let me know."

Lizzie nodded, though she had no intention of involving him further. "Thank you, Detective. I'll keep that in mind."

Powers lingered for a moment, studying her face as if trying to discern the truth. Lastly, he tipped his hat again. "Be careful, Miss Yoder. Sometimes, these things escalate."

As he walked back to his car, Lizzie closed the door and leaned against it, her nerves rattled. The impact of the warning on the window pressed worryingly on her, but she pushed the fear aside. There was too much at stake for her to back down now.

When Evert arrived a short while later, he immediately noticed the spray-painted words. His jaw tightened as he stepped inside the shop. "What happened?"

Lizzie shook her head, her voice low. "Someone's... I'm sure it's Amos just trying to scare me. But I won't let him."

Evert frowned, his expression dark. "You know this means we're on the right track."

Lizzie nodded. "I know," she mouthed the words more than spoke them. "But I already told Detective Powers it's probably just a prank."

Evert's head snapped toward her. "He was here?" His voice rose, and Lizzie winced at the intensity.

"Someone must have called it in."

Evert took a deep breath, running a hand through his dark hair. "This isn't just some Amish squabble. You can't ignore this."

Lizzie's lips tightened. "I'm not ignoring it."

Evert paced the length of the shop, his boots scuffing the wooden floor. "What if whoever did this doesn't stop at threats? What if they decide to hurt you?"

Lizzie swallowed hard. She hated the fear gnawing at the edges of her confidence, but she refused to let it consume her. "I'm not afraid," she said dimly, though her voice lacked conviction.

Evert stopped pacing and turned to face her, his expression serious. "Maybe you're not, but you should be. Whoever did this knows what we're digging into. They know about your grandmother, about the yarn, about the accounts. They're trying to silence you, Lizzie."

"What would you have me do, Evert? Allow the police to barge into the community? Let them interrogate everyone and make things worse?"

"Yes, if that's what it takes to keep you safe, then yes."

Lizzie's eyes flashed with frustration. "You don't

understand. If I involve the police, it'll put a spotlight on *Simply Yarn*, on my grandmother's memory, on everything. The community will turn their backs on me. My shop might not survive the backlash."

Evert stepped closer, his voice softening. "Your grandmother wouldn't have wanted you to put yourself in danger. This isn't about what the community thinks, it's about the truth."

Her shoulders sagged, and she let out a weary sigh. "And what if the truth destroys everything?"

Evert crossed his arms and leaned back. "Sometimes, the truth is the only thing that can set things right."

Lizzie met his gaze, searching his face for reassurance. She wanted to believe him, to trust that he was right, but the burden of the decision pressed severely on her. "I'll think about it," she said finally. "But for now, I'm not calling the detective back."

Evert nodded, though the tension in his jaw remained.

The rhythmic squeak of a razor blade filled the air as Evert scraped on one end of the window and Lizzie on the other. The black paint flaked off in long threads before it came off, eventually leaving smudged streaks against their efforts.

Neither spoke as the tension of the morning lingered between them.

Ultimately, after what felt like hours but was only minutes, the glass gleamed again. Lizzie wiped her hands on her apron and turned the *Open* sign over, signaling the shop's readiness for business. She glanced at Evert, who was leaning on the window frame, his expression distant.

"So," she began, breaking the silence, "what brought you here in the first place? It couldn't have been just to help me scrape windows."

Evert blinked, as though pulled from a memory. "*Ach*, that's right." He straightened, running a hand through his hair. "I wanted to tell you something. A memory, actually."

Lizzie tilted her head, curiosity flickering in her eyes. "What kind of memory?"

Evert shifted his weight, hesitating before speaking. "It's about my grandmother. She didn't knit or crochet, but she always stopped by *Simply Yarn* to see your grandmother the first of every month. It sticks out in my mind because she never bought anything, and when she went for a visit, we'd go to the cottage."

Lizzie frowned, leaning against the counter. "Why do you

think she came, then? Besides being friends?"

"That's what I've been wondering," Evert admitted. "I don't remember her ever carrying any supplies home. And it wasn't just about visiting, either. They'd always go into the back room and talk, just the two of them. At the time, I didn't think much of it; adults always seemed to have their own mysterious business. But now…"

"Now it seems odd," Lizzie finished for him. "Especially if she didn't crochet or knit."

Evert nodded. "Afterwards, though, she always made the trip special. She'd take me for an ice cream cone at the *Dairy Bar* or let me pick out a bag of candy at the *Mercantile*. It was like she was trying to distract me or make me forget she'd spent so much time in the shop."

Lizzie's gaze softened. "It sounds like she cared about you deeply. Those small things like ice cream and candy were her way of showing love."

Evert chuckled, but the sound was tinged with regret. "*Jah*, she did. And I gave her so much trouble in return. When I was a teenager, I was… I wasn't the easiest to deal with."

Lizzie smiled faintly, sensing the weight behind his words. "Most teenagers aren't. But your grandparents raised you as their own, didn't they? That says a lot."

He nodded gradually, his expression clouding. "They did. And now I understand why things always felt... distant. They were keeping that secret from me. It was always there, unspoken but present. Looking back, I can see it now."

"But they loved you. That much is clear, Evert. Secrets don't erase love."

"I just wish I could find my parents. I need to know why they left me. Why did they disappear? Maybe then I'd at last understand."

Lizzie's heart ached at the raw emotion in his voice. "You'll find them. I don't know how, but I believe you will."

They stood in the quiet shop for a moment, the hum of the morning settling around them. Evert straightened, exhaling intensely. "*Jah.*"

Ella walked up, her shoulders hunched against the morning chill. She glanced around before offering Lizzie a small, shy smile.

"*Goot meiya,*" Ella greeted, she muttered.

Lizzie nodded warmly as they went inside. "I've got a few things for you to work on this morning if you don't mind."

Ella nodded immediately, folding her hands in front of her. "Of course."

Lizzie gestured toward a stack of boxes near the counter. "Those need to be unpacked and sorted. And I thought the display on the back wall could use some rearranging. Maybe put the patterns and knitting needles together so it's easier for customers to find what they need."

"*Jah*, I can do that," Ella said, her voice steadier now with direction. She moved toward the boxes, her movements deliberate but still hesitant.

Lizzie watched her momentarily, then hesitated as a thought struck her. "Ella?"

The young woman paused, her hand hovering over the first box. "*Jah*?"

Lizzie stepped closer, her expression curious but kind. "I've been meaning to ask… why was Amos at your uncle's shop the other day?"

Ella froze, her back stiffening. She didn't turn around, but Lizzie could see her knuckles whiten as she gripped the box. "I… uh… I don't know," she stammered.

Lizzie tilted her head, studying her carefully. "It's just…they don't seem like the kind of men who'd have much in common. Are they friends?"

Ella turned deliberately, her face pale and her eyes darting nervously. "I don't think they're friends. Uncle Jacob doesn't talk much about him, but he does occasionally stop by the shop."

Evert frowned. "But they were meeting that day? Do you know why?"

Ella swallowed hard, her gaze dropping to the floor. "I'm not sure. Uncle Jacob doesn't tell me everything."

Before Evert could press further, Lizzie's voice broke the tense silence. "We're scaring the poor girl," she said, stepping into the conversation with a lopsided grin. "Not everyone's as eager to dive into a mystery as we are."

Evert turned, his frown softening. "We're not trying to scare you."

"Let's ease up on the detective routine," Lizzie teased, her tone light. She turned to Ella, her expression softening. "Don't mind us, we're just curious... you know, the kind that doesn't rest until we've got all the answers."

Ella's lips twitched into a small, hesitant smile. "It's... okay."

As Ella turned back to her task, her movements less rigid

than before, Lizzie shot Evert a curious look. She shook her head, trying to quiet her mind about the whole situation.

As Evert pushed away from the counter, he adjusted his jacket and glanced toward the door. "Well, I'd better get going. Isaiah's got me helping at the buggy shop this morning. I think he's trying to work me to the bone."

Lizzie smirked, setting down a clipboard she'd been holding. "Or maybe he's just keeping you out of trouble."

Evert laughed. "Could be that too. But hey..." He hesitated for a moment, his hand resting on the doorframe. "If you're free later, how about grabbing lunch? I know a place in town that makes a better toasted cheese sandwich than I do."

Lizzie blinked, surprised by the invitation. "Lunch?"

Despite herself, Lizzie felt her cheeks warm. She glanced at the clock, noting the time. "I guess Ella can handle things for an hour or so."

Evert's grin widened. "Great. I'll swing by around noon. My treat."

Lizzie shook her head, but a small smile tugged at her lips. "You don't have to... "

"I insist," Evert said, his voice light but firm. "Think of it as thanks for letting me stick around and dig through your grandmother's secrets."

She chuckled softly, the tension from earlier melting away. "All right. Noon it is."

Evert tipped his ball cap. "I'll see you then."

As the door shut behind him, Lizzie caught herself smiling. She instantly busied herself organizing the counter. Still, the thought of lunch with Evert lingered on her mind, leaving a strange mix of butterflies in her stomach she hadn't anticipated.

***

The familiar chime of the bell above the door at *The Restaurant on the Corner* greeted Lizzie and Evert as they stepped inside. The cozy space was alive with the low hum of conversations and the comforting clink of cutlery against plates.

A cheerful waitress approached them, her name tag reading *Abigail*. Lizzie recognized her immediately as the same girl who had served her and her grandmother on that fateful day.

"Lizzie," Abigail said, her voice warm but carrying a tinge of sadness. "It's good to see you. I was so sorry to hear about Esther. She was one of my favorite customers."

"Thanks," Lizzie replied, managing a faint smile. "She loved it here."

Abigail nodded, her expression genuine. "Would you like your usual table by the window?"

Lizzie hesitated, glancing at Evert. He gave her a small nod, and she agreed. As they followed Abigail to the table, Lizzie couldn't help but notice the subtle pang of loss that struck her as they sat in the same spot she and her grandmother had shared just weeks before.

After handing them menus, Abigail lingered for a moment. "Do you need a few minutes to decide?"

Evert shook his head. "We'll just have the lunch special, tomato soup, and toasted cheese, please."

"Sure thing," Abigail said, jotting down the order. Then, as she turned to leave, Lizzie called out.

"Abigail, wait."

The waitress paused, looking back expectantly.

"That day... when I was here with my grandmother... what tea did she have?" Lizzie asked, her tone careful.

Abigail nodded immediately. "Esther brought her own blend that day. I just brought her hot water, while she waited on you to arrive. It was super busy that day and I was glad you were late in joining her."

Lizzie exchanged a glance with Evert as Abigail walked away.

Lizzie thought for a moment, then shook her head. "I remember her mentioning that it tasted a little off. She didn't seem too concerned about it." Lizzie's stomach twisted. "That just doesn't sit right with me now."

Evert's expression was grim. "And the fact that she brought her own tea makes it even stranger. Someone would've had to tamper with it beforehand."

Lizzie shook her head, her fingers tracing the rim of the glass. "But how? And why?"

Evert leaned back in his chair; his arms crossed. "Someone wanted her gone, Lizzie. I hate to say it, but this doesn't sound like natural causes. Between the notes, the ledger, and now this…" He trailed off, his jaw tightening.

Lizzie looked out the window, her thoughts swirling. "Abigail said it was busy that day. Whoever did this could've easily gone unnoticed."

Evert sipped his water and added, "I think we need to figure out what she was drinking that day. Maybe visiting *Jacob's Herb Shop* will give us some answers."

Tracy Fredrychowski

CHAPTER 8

L izzie and Evert stepped into *Jacob's Herb Shop*, the scent of dried rose petals and chamomile wafting toward them. The small shop was lined with shelves overflowing with jars of herbs, efficiently labeled by Jacob. The air was warm, almost stifling, but Lizzie didn't mind. She was determined to get answers.

Jacob looked up from behind the counter, his glasses perched low on his nose as he scribbled something into a ledger. "Lizzie, Evert," he greeted with a nod, though his voice carried an edge of caution. "What can I do for you?"

Lizzie approached the counter, glancing at Evert before speaking. "I was hoping you could tell me about the tea mixture my grandmother used to get from you. She was drinking it the day she passed, and I'd like to know what was in it."

Jacob blinked, his pen pausing mid-stroke. "Her tea? *Ach*, well, she always liked her chamomile and mint blend, sometimes with a bit of valerian root if she was having trouble sleeping." He hesitated, scratching his beard. "But I don't recall exactly what was in her last order."

Lizzie frowned. "You don't keep records?"

Jacob shifted uncomfortably, glancing at a stack of papers on the counter. "Normally, I do. But... " He stopped, looking genuinely flustered. "I had a stack of invoices go missing a few days ago. I've been trying to piece them back together, but..." His voice trailed off, and he gestured helplessly to the disorganized pile.

Evert folded his arms, his tone skeptical. "Missing invoices? That's convenient."

Jacob shot him a sharp look but promptly turned his attention back to Lizzie. "I can tell you what she usually ordered, but I can't say for certain what was in her last mix." He rubbed the back of his neck, clearly uneasy. "The truth is, Ella mixed her last batch for her. She's been helping with some of the simple orders."

"Ella?" Lizzie asked, her voice softening. "Did she mix anything different that day?"

Jacob shrugged. "Not that I recall. Esther was a creature of habit. Do you have any of the tea left at her cottage? If you bring it by, I can figure out what was in it."

Lizzie shook her head. "I've searched the entire house and found no container with loose tea."

Jacob's brow furrowed, and he looked down at the counter, tapping his pen absently. "Strange. She always kept a good supply on hand. It's not like her to run out."

Evert leaned against the counter, his sharp gaze fixed on Jacob. "You're sure you don't remember anything else? Maybe something unusual about her order?"

Jacob's hand tightened around the pen, and he shifted again, avoiding Evert's eyes. "I told you everything I know. Let me know if you find the tea, and I'll figure it out for you."

Lizzie nodded, though a sense of unease gnawed at her. "*Denki.* If I come across anything, I'll bring it to you."

As they turned to leave, Evert murmured under his breath, "Something's not right here. He's hiding something."

Lizzie didn't respond, but the sinking feeling in her chest told her Evert was probably right.

***

As the door swung closed, Jacob exhaled a shaky breath. He

leaned clumsily against the counter, his hands gripping the edge as if it were the only thing holding him upright. His chest felt tight, and his pulse raced as the weight of their questions settled over him.

The tea. The invoices. The herbs.

With a glance toward the door to ensure Lizzie and Evert were on their way, Jacob straightened and began riffling through the disorganized stack of papers on his counter. His movements were frantic, the usually methodical man now reduced to a bundle of nerves.

"Where are they?" he muttered under his breath, shoving aside an empty jar and a clipboard. "They were here last month. I know they were."

He moved to the small office in the back of the shop, where another pile of receipts and invoices lay scattered across the desk. Pulling open drawers with sharp, jerky movements, Jacob sifted through the clutter. Every sheet he handled made his frustration grow; none of them were the ones he was looking for.

The missing invoices and the specialty herbs he had ordered; ones not listed in his usual stock inventory were gone. Completely gone.

Jacob clenched his fists, the veins in his forearms bulging. *If they end up in the wrong hands...* he didn't even finish the thought. The consequences were too severe to dwell on.

Turning back to the shelves where he stored his private supply of herbs, he checked the jars one by one, pulling them down to peer inside. Some were mislabeled intentionally, a precaution he thought would ensure his secret blends. His mind immediately went to Ella. She had access to the shop when he wasn't there. Had she moved the invoices? Or worse, had Amos been snooping around again?

If Amos got hold of those invoices, he could use them against him. The thought made Jacob's jaw tighten. Amos Zook was a shadow that lingered too close, his plans always threatening to pull Jacob deeper into trouble. It had been a mistake trusting him, a mistake Jacob now realized might cost him everything, his shop, his reputation, and possibly Ella's future.

"Ella," he whispered, his voice laced with both guilt and fear. He hated dragging her into this mess, but the reality was she was already part of it, whether she knew it or not. His involvement with Amos was no secret to her, though he did his best to shield her from the worst of it.

Jacob's hands trembled as he grabbed the remaining invoices on the desk, flipping through them in desperation. He paused on one, his heart sinking as he recognized the supplier's name. *Wholesale Herbs & Tinctures.* It was one of Amos's connections, a supplier Jacob had reluctantly ordered from under pressure.

But now it was missing. The invoice he needed to cover his tracks, to explain the orders, if anyone asked, was gone.

Jacob raked a hand through his thinning hair, muttering a prayer under his breath. "*Gott*, if You can hear me, I need help. I've made a mess of things, and I don't know how to fix it."

The sound of the bell above the door startled him, and he instantly straightened, forcing a calm expression onto his face as a customer entered the shop. But inside, the storm was far from settled.

***

Later that evening, Lizzie sat in the quiet of her grandmother's cottage. The day had been long, filled with more questions than answers, and as the rain pattered gently against the windows, she found herself drawn back to her grandmother's journal. It rested on the side table, inviting her into its pages.

Taking a deep breath, Lizzie reached for the journal and opened it to the page she'd bookmarked earlier. The familiar scrawl of her grandmother's handwriting greeted her like an old friend, each curve of the letters evoking a pang of longing. Yet, as she read, the words painted a picture of inner turmoil she hadn't expected.

"How much can one heart bear? The responsibility of secrets grows heavier each day, but is it not better to protect those I love than to expose them to the world's judgment?"

Lizzie read on, her grandmother's words laced with an uncharacteristic hesitance.

"Deceit has cost so much, but what will happen if the truth is laid bare? And Jacob... poor Jacob, his heart was too eager to trust Amos's promises. Now, he teeters on the edge, his debts piling higher than the shop shelves."

Lizzie's heart tightened at the mention of Jacob. She'd sensed his unease earlier in the day, but her grandmother's words painted a more dire picture. Jacob's financial struggles weren't just a passing hardship, they were a precarious thread in a web of larger secrets.

"But at what cost?" the next line read, written in bold, deliberate strokes. *"Must my silence condemn one to protect the other? The truth is like a storm on the horizon; I can see it coming, but I do not know how to stop it."*

Lizzie closed her eyes for a moment, her fingers lightly brushing over the page. The words felt heavy, almost too much to process. Her grandmother had always seemed so steadfast, so unwavering in her convictions. But here, in the privacy of her journal, she had wrestled with decisions that could shatter the fragile peace of Willow Springs.

Turning another page, Lizzie found a brief but chilling entry: *"The cost of silence is steep, but the cost of truth may be steeper. Can E's future endure the bulk of what I know? Can I live with myself if I let them destroy him?"*

E? Lizzie's pulse quickened. Her grandmother had mentioned "E" before, in the ledger and now here. It had to mean Evert. But why? What role did he play in all of this?

The final lines on the page stopped Lizzie cold: *"The truth will come to light. It always does. But Gott forgive me, I cannot be the one to reveal it. I only pray it reaches the right hands when the time comes."*

Lizzie closed the journal, her hands trembling. The weight

of her grandmother's words hung in the air, a solemn reminder that the answers she sought were tied to decisions made long before her time.

She glanced toward the window, where the rain continued to fall in steady streams. Outside, the world seemed as gray and uncertain as the path ahead. But one thing was clear: Her grandmother had carried these burdens alone for too long. Now it was Lizzie's turn to uncover the truth and perhaps face the storm her grandmother had seen coming.

Lizzie set her grandmother's journal aside. She leaned back against the chair, the flickering oil lamp dancing shadows on the room's walls. The faint scent of autumn from her quilt that had hung on the line all day wrapped around her, a bittersweet reminder of the hands that had stitched it. Her mind raced with everything she had uncovered over the past few weeks, threads of questions tangling and knotting together until she didn't know where one ended and another began.

She couldn't let it go. Not yet.

Her grandmother's cryptic words haunted her: *E's future. Justice for E. The cost of silence.* Lizzie squeezed her eyes shut, willing the phrases to unlock their secrets. What had her grandmother known? What had she been trying to protect, or reveal?

The journal wasn't the only clue. There was the ledger she'd found in the desk, its columns filled with deposits that made no sense. And why had they stopped twelve years ago and why hadn't there been a recent bank statement? Lizzie thought of Evert's troubled expression when she'd shown him the entries. His name seemed tied to the mystery, but even he didn't have answers.

The crochet bag came to mind next. The synthetic yarn she'd discovered was still tucked inside, its fibers nothing like the yarn her grandmother always preferred. And that pattern, so geometric, so unlike anything she'd ever seen her grandmother make. Mrs. Bricker had confirmed the yarn was fake, and Amos Zook's name kept surfacing. Yet here she was, piecing together a puzzle that seemed to lead straight to him.

Her thoughts drifted to the warning to "stop digging," chilling her more than she cared to admit. And the note. And Erie… why had it been postmarked from there? What connection could her grandmother, a *Plain* woman with deep roots in Willow Springs, possibly have to a city hours away?

Then there was Jacob. She couldn't ignore the smoldering invoices she and Evert had found in his burning barrel or the tea her grandmother had been drinking the day she died. Jacob's flustered reaction when she asked about the tea only raised more questions. Ella's nervous behavior only added to her unease.

Lizzie sat up straighter, pulling her quilt closer as a chill crept through her. And how could her grandmother's tea... her own tea, now missing, have played a role in her sudden death?

She ran a hand through her still-damp hair from an earlier shower, frustration bubbling up. It was too much.

Her gaze drifted to the journal resting on the end table. "What were you trying to tell me, *Grossmommi?*" she whispered, her voice thin as air as she walked to her bed. *Everything is so confusing...* she thought.

The wind howled outside, and the flicker of the lamp's flame seemed to mimic the restless swirl of her thoughts. Lizzie crawled under her blankets and stared at the ceiling as her mind circled back to the same question: Who can I trust?

The image of Evert flashed in her mind, his steady presence, his unrelenting search for answers, his quiet moments of vulnerability. She wanted to believe in him, but the shadow of his past loomed large.

And Ella... sweet, nervous Ella, whose eyes darted every time Amos's name came up. Was she protecting Jacob, or was there something more?

Lizzie sighed, pulling the quilt up to her chin. She had prayed for clarity, but all she found was more questions. Sleep wouldn't come easily tonight.

***

Evert leaned against the counter in the buggy shop's workshop, the scent of sawdust and oil hanging in the air. Isaiah wiped his hands on a rag, eyeing his cousin warily.

"You're quieter than usual tonight," Isaiah added, tossing the rag onto the workbench.

Evert stared at the floor for a moment before looking up. "It's all starting to feel connected, but I can't figure out how. Amos Zook, the yarn shop in Erie, the bank account Esther left behind, none of it makes sense. And now..." He paused, his voice low and simmering. "I've been talking to people... at least those who will give me the time of day. I found out Amos was my father's best friend at one time."

Isaiah's brow furrowed. "Amos? That can't be right. He's never mentioned anything about that."

"Of course he hasn't," Evert snapped. "Why would he? If

Amos is the key to everything I've been searching for, he's not going to make it easy. He's up to something, I know it. Esther knew it too. She was threatening to expose him before she died."

Isaiah leaned back against the workbench, his expression thoughtful. "You think Amos had something to do with your parents leaving? I thought we figured they left because of you. The baby born out of wedlock."

Evert shrugged, but frustration seeped into his voice. "It's possible. Everything about my parents is a dead end. No records, no trace. It's like they vanished. The more I dig, the more it feels like they changed their names to cover their tracks. And now, every road I take keeps leading back to Amos."

Isaiah sighed, crossing his arms. "If that's true, you need to be careful. Amos doesn't take kindly to people poking around in his business. You've seen how he operates."

"I'm not scared of him," Evert said firmly. "But I don't trust him either. That's why I don't want Lizzie involved in this part. Amos has already been harassing her, and I'm not dragging her further into this mess."

Isaiah gave a small nod of approval. "Good. But what are you planning to do? Confront him outright?"

"Not yet," Evert replied. "First, I need to figure out how deep this goes. I want to know why Amos and my father were so close, and what made my parents feel they could stay or take me with them. Esther knew something... something big. I just need to piece it together."

Isaiah frowned. "You're walking a fine line. If Amos catches wind of what you're digging for, he's not going to sit back and watch. You've got to be smart about this."

Evert nodded reluctantly, running a hand through his hair. "I know. But I can't just sit here and wait for answers to fall into my lap."

Isaiah studied him for a moment before speaking again, his tone softer. "What if it just leads to more questions, or worse, more pain?"

Evert's jaw tightened, but his eyes held a flicker of vulnerability. "It's already painful. Not knowing, not understanding why they left me behind... That's what hurts the most. I'd rather face the truth, no matter how hard it is, than live with this hole in my chest."

Isaiah nodded, his gaze steady. "Then you'd better be ready for whatever you find."

As Evert pushed himself off the counter and headed for the

door, Isaiah called after him. "And be careful with Amos. He's not the type to forgive and forget."

Evert gave a small wave without turning back. "I'll keep that in mind."

Stepping into the cool evening air, Evert took a deep breath, his thoughts churning. Amos Zook was more than just a shady businessman; he was a link to the parents.

Tracy Fredrychowski

CHAPTER 9

The room was dim, lit only by a single window facing the east. The smell of dust and old paper filled the air as Evert entered Amos Zook's office. It wasn't a welcoming space; cold, cluttered, and intentionally uninviting. Shelves crammed with ledgers, faded invoices, and samples of product lined the walls. A large desk dominated the center of the room, its surface buried under stacks of papers and boxes.

Amos looked up, startled, as Evert shut the door behind him. His hand paused mid-shuffle over a stack of receipts. For a split second, his eyes narrowed, but he abruptly masked his surprise.

"What do you want, Miller?" Amos asked, his voice gruff and wary. He leaned back in his chair, a forced calm settling over his features.

Evert stepped forward, his boots echoing on the wooden floor. He didn't bother sitting down. "You know why I'm here."

Amos raised an eyebrow. "Do I?"

"I want to know what you know about my parents."

The room seemed to grow colder. Amos's lips pressed into a thin line, and his gaze flickered to the papers on his desk. "I don't know what you're talking about."

Evert's jaw tightened. "Don't lie to me. I know you knew them. What I don't know is how you're connected to them, why their names keep coming up, and why everything I uncover ties back to you."

Amos chuckled dryly, a sound without humor. "You've got a vivid imagination, boy. I'd be careful with it if I were you."

Evert leaned on the desk, his eyes burning into Amos's. "They're gone. They left me behind and disappeared. But you? You're still here, still tied to whatever mess they were involved in. What are you hiding?"

Amos stood abruptly, his chair scraping against the floor. His face was a mask of anger, but there was something else there too... fear. "I don't owe you any answers. Your parents made their choices. They left the community. They left you. If you want someone to blame, look at them, not me."

Evert didn't back down. "You know why they left. Tell me the truth."

For a moment, Amos was silent, his hand gripping the edge

of the desk so hard his knuckles turned white. Then he spoke, his voice laced with tension. "The truth is dangerous, Miller. You'd be wise to leave it buried. Your parents walked away from this life, and they took things they shouldn't have. If you dig too deep, you'll find things you won't like."

Evert's stomach churned. "What things?"

Amos grinned, his courage returning. "If you don't stop poking your nose where it doesn't belong, you'll regret it. That's a promise."

The air between them crackled with tension. Evert knew pushing further wouldn't get him anywhere, but Amos's slip had confirmed one thing. He knew more than he was letting on.

Without another word, Evert turned and walked out of the office, his mind racing.

***

As soon as Evert's truck roared out of the gravel driveway, Amos reached for the bishop-approved business phone and dialed. His hands trembled as he paced the small office, his boots scuffing against the worn floorboards.

The line clicked, and a man's weary voice answered. "What

is it now, Amos?"

"Evert Miller," Amos barked. "He's been sniffing around, asking questions about Nathan and Rebecca. He was just here."

There was silence on the other end of the line, then a sharp intake of breath. "Did you tell him anything?"

"Of course not," Amos snapped. "But he's not giving up. He knows too much already."

The man's voice lowered, tinged with frustration. "I thought we agreed this was over. He was supposed to stay out of this."

"Well, he didn't," Amos growled. "And now he's poking his nose where it doesn't belong. If he finds out the truth, you're finished."

"You're the one who brought us into this mess," the man shot back. "All we wanted was a clean break."

"A clean break?" Amos laughed bitterly. "You took something that didn't belong to you, and now it's catching up to you."

"Do you think he knows about the money?" the man asked, his voice tight with fear.

Amos paused, his jaw clenching. "Not yet. But it's only a matter of time. You'd better figure out how to handle this, because if he finds that account, you're on your own."

The line went dead, leaving Amos standing alone in the dim office, his mind racing. If Evert kept digging, Amos would have to take matters into his own hands.

***

The herb shop was quiet that morning, the scent of mint and lavender lingering in the air as Ella busied herself behind the counter, sorting jars and wiping down shelves. Her movements were quick and precise, but her anxious glances toward the door didn't escape Jacob's notice.

"You'd best head over to Lizzie's," Jacob said, not unkindly, as he folded his arms and leaned against the counter.

Ella hesitated, her fingers nervously twisting together. "Do you need anything before I go?"

Jacob shook his head, offering a faint smile. "*Nee*, just get along now. I'll manage here."

Ella nodded and gathered her shawl. "I'll come back for lunch."

Before she could leave, the bell over the door jingled sharply. The sight of Amos standing in the doorway made Ella freeze. Amos's dark eyes swept the room, landing on her with a smug grin that sent a chill down her spine.

"Morning, Jacob. And little Miss Ella." Amos's voice was smooth, almost mocking.

Jacob's jaw tightened. "Ella was just leaving."

Amos chuckled, stepping aside to let her pass. "Don't let me keep you. Run along now. Adults have business to discuss."

Ella hurried past him without a word, her steps quick as she vanished out the door. Jacob waited until the door swung shut before turning his glare to Amos.

"What do you want?"

Amos strolled further into the shop, his boots clicking against the floor. He let his hand drift over a shelf of painstakingly labeled jars, plucking one down to inspect it. "Nice setup you've got here. Shame if something were to happen to it."

"Spit it out," Jacob growled. "I'm not in the mood for your games."

Amos smirked and set the jar back down with exaggerated care. "Touchy today, are we? Fine, I'll get to the point. Evert Miller's return is stirring up trouble. I need him gone."

Jacob frowned. "What's he got to do with anything? He's just trying to piece together his past."

Amos's expression darkened. "And that's exactly the problem. Evert's digging where he shouldn't. He's poking his nose into things that were supposed to stay buried. You, me, if he keeps asking questions, he'll uncover more than he bargained for. And if I go down, you're going down with me."

Jacob swallowed hard, his throat dry. "What do you expect me to do about it?"

Amos leaned closer, his voice dropping to a dangerous whisper. "Find a way to get him out of town. I don't care how you do it, but make sure he doesn't stick around. Or I'll be making some calls."

Jacob stiffened. "What calls?"

Amos grinned, but there was no warmth in it. "To a certain person who I hear has been looking for your sweet little niece. You wouldn't want him to know where she's hiding, would you?"

Jacob gasped. "You leave Ella out of this."

Amos raised an eyebrow. "That's up to you. Keep her safe by doing what I say. Otherwise..." He trailed off, letting the threat hang in the air. Amos picked up a bottle of herbs and continued. "You have everything you need at your fingertips to ensure he disappears for good." He replaced the bottle on the shelf and added, "And don't forget if he finds out how deeply you're involved with smuggling those toxic herbs to the black market, you'll go down right with the whole operation, for sure and certain."

Jacob stared at the man, his mind racing at the thought of what he'd let himself get mixed up with.

Amos laughed, a low, cold sound. "Those herbs are quite the insurance policy."

Jacob's heart sank. He'd been careful, so careful. But Amos had a way of twisting the truth to suit his needs. "You're bluffing."

"Am I?" Amos asked, his grin widened. "You think the good folks of Willow Springs will side with you once I show them the evidence? If he keeps sniffing around... well that boy's persistence is a liability."

Jacob ran a hand over his face, Amos's threats pressing down on him. "Why should I trust you? You're just as likely to throw me under the buggy as anyone else."

Amos shrugged. "That's a risk you'll have to take. But you've got a choice here, Jacob. Help me get rid of Evert, and I'll make sure this all goes away. Refuse, and... well, let's just say things won't go so smoothly for you or your dear niece."

Jacob stared at the man, his thoughts swirling in a chaotic storm. Amos had backed him into a corner, and the stakes were higher than ever. But one thing was clear: Evert's presence in Willow Springs was shaking loose secrets that had been hidden for far too long.

Ella had stayed in the shadows just outside the open shop window. She heard every threatening word Amos had spat at her uncle. His words left her stomach reeling as she found unrestrained relief in a nearby bush.

***

Ella fidgeted with the skein of yarn in her hands, her fingers working the fibers absently as she tried to steady her racing thoughts. Lizzie had given her clear instructions about rearranging the knitting needles and updating the display of pattern books on the back wall, but Ella found herself distracted. Her mind drifted back to the herb shop and the tense exchange with her uncle.

She hated the way Amos always seemed to tower over her uncle, his presence a dark cloud that left the air heavy and suffocating. The moment Amos had entered the shop earlier, her uncle had waved her off, his eyes darting nervously toward Amos as if to silently plead with her to leave. It wasn't the first time he'd done that, and Ella suspected it wouldn't be the last.

She adjusted the pattern books on the shelf, forcing herself to focus, but the memory of Amos's sneer wouldn't leave her. She could still hear his gruff voice cutting through the air, his words sharp and loaded with menace.

Ella hated feeling powerless. It was the same feeling she'd had back in Wisconsin, the same helplessness that had driven her to leave everything she knew behind. She tucked the thought away quickly, afraid that if she lingered on it too long, it would appear on her face.

Lizzie's voice startled her, pulling her from her thoughts. "Ella, could you grab me those skeins of yarn from the counter?" Lizzie asked, motioning toward a pile of new arrivals.

Ella nodded, scurrying toward the counter. She felt Lizzie's eyes on her, watching her with a curiosity that made her stomach twist. Ella knew Lizzie was kind, but she couldn't help feeling as if Lizzie saw too much, as if she could see right through her painstakingly constructed walls.

As she handed the yarn over, Lizzie hesitated, her gaze

lingering. "Is something bothering you today?" Lizzie's tone was gentle, but it carried a note of curiosity that made Ella's heart skip.

"*Nee*," Ella replied, her voice a little too bright.

"You know I'm here if you ever want to talk. You seem distracted this morning. Are you sure nothing is bothering you?"

The question sent a jolt of panic through Ella. She thought she'd gotten good at hiding her fears, but looking at Lizzie, she sensed her friend could see right through her. "I guess I'm just a little worried about my uncle today. Amos stopped in again and he upsets him so."

Lizzie frowned. "What's the hold that man has over everyone in this town?"

Ella felt the walls closing in. Her throat tightened, and she couldn't bring herself to meet Lizzie's gaze. She busied herself with rearranging the yarn, her movements quick and jerky as she tried to hide just how concerning Amos's visit was.

The bell above the door jingled as Evert walked in, his easy smile lighting up the room. "Morning, ladies," he said, his voice a welcome distraction from Lizzie's questions.

Ella's nerves settled a little as the attention shifted to Evert.

He had a way of lightening the mood, even if his presence still made her uneasy. She caught herself glancing at him out of the corner of her eye, wondering if he could see through her too.

"Don't let us stop you," Evert said, gesturing toward the shelves Ella was working on. "You seem busy."

"I… I am," Ella replied, her voice shaky. She turned back to her task, grateful for the excuse to avoid further conversation.

As the tension in the room eased, Lizzie laughed lightly at something Evert said, her tone warm and relaxed. Ella glanced back at them, a pang of envy twisting in her chest. She wished she could be that at ease and shed the weight pressing down on her.

How did Amos know? She had confided in Esther, but she was certain her old friend would have never revealed the extent of her past to anyone. Amos could end her life in Willow Springs with just one phone call.

Ella turned back to the shelves, determined to keep her head down. She hated feeling so out of control, but for now, all she could do was keep going and pray that her past wouldn't catch up to her.

The soft hum of Lizzie and Evert's conversation across the

shop barely registered as Ella arranged skeins of yarn into neat rows. Her hands worked mechanically, the vibrant colors blending into a blur as her mind drifted to the memory she wished she could erase.

It felt as if it had happened just yesterday, the day her world tilted on its axis...

She'd been cleaning Ura's family home with his sister as part of the preparations for church service. The air lingered of lemon polish and wood shavings, the usual comforting scents of an Amish home. Yet that day, everything felt off.

Ura's schwester had stepped out to tend to the garden, leaving Ella alone in Ura's room. It was tidy, almost unnaturally so, but a hint of his blacksmithing job filled her nose. Ella's eyes wandered as she dusted his dresser. That's when she saw it... a small drawer left partially open.

It wasn't her place to pry, but an unshakable feeling compelled her. With trembling hands, she pulled it open.

She first noticed a stack of strange invoices and recent letters from a woman bound together with a piece of fraying twine. She unfolded the first letter, her breath catching as her eyes scanned the words that revealed a side of Ura she didn't know.

Ella's hands shook as she shoved everything back into the drawer. Her stomach churned, bile rising in her throat as the realization hit her that this was the man her father and the bishop had chosen for her, the man they insisted was Gott-fearing and respectable.

The memory shifted to the confrontation. She had waited until they were alone, her voice trembling as she brought up what she had found.

"Ura," she had begun cautiously, "I need to ask you about something I saw when cleaning your room."

His eyes darkened immediately, his face twisting into a scowl. "What were you doing snooping around my things?"

"I found letters and invoices," she continued, her voice fading before it fully formed. "The letters from that woman? They're not proper."

Ura's response was instant and violent. He grabbed her arm tightly, his fingers digging into her flesh. "You had no right to go through my things," he spat, his voice low and menacing. "You're going to be my fraa, and your place is to trust me. Don't question me; my business is no concern of yours... not now and certainly won't be once we're married."

The bruise he left on her arm lasted for days, but the fear he instilled in her lasted far longer. Ella had never felt so small, so powerless.

She had tried to tell her father, to explain why she couldn't marry Ura Hostetler, but her words fell on deaf ears. The bishop had already given his blessing, and her father saw Ura as a good match and a hard worker who could provide for her well. Speaking out felt like screaming into a void.

She prayed Ura would change, but after two months of continued harsh treatment at his hands, the decision to leave came quickly. Her father, sensing her distress but refusing to confront the truth, secretly sent her to live with Jacob in Willow Springs. Delaying the marriage was their only option without bringing shame to their family.

"Ella?"

Lizzie's voice snapped her back to the present. Ella blinked rapidly, realizing she had been clutching a skein of yarn so forcefully it was beginning to unravel.

"Are you all right?" Lizzie asked, her tone laced with concern.

Ella forced a smile, nodding. "*Jah*, I'm fine," she replied, her voice tight.

She turned away, pretending to rearrange the display, but

her heart pounded in her chest. Too many people knew her secret: her father, Jacob, and even Esther. And now, Amos was using it against her. She hated feeling so out of control, but what scared her most was the thought of being sent back to Wisconsin, to Ura, and the life she had narrowly escaped.

As she worked, she stole a glance at Evert and Lizzie, their easy camaraderie, a stark contrast to the storm brewing inside her. Ella clenched her jaw, vowing to keep her secret buried. No one else could know.

CHAPTER 10

The soft hiss of the oil lamp added light to the small sitting room in Lizzie's cottage. The yarn her grandmother had left behind lay in her lap, a skein of deep green threaded between her fingers. Lizzie sat cross-legged on the worn sofa, the crochet bag at her side, and the handwritten pattern spread out on the small table in front of her. The flowery script caught the light, the letters looping gracefully across the page. It was still so familiar but not of her grandmother's style.

Lizzie picked up her crochet hook and let her hands move instinctively, picking up where her grandmother had left off. The yarn slid between her fingers, soft and pliable, as she followed the instructions on the delicate page. Each stitch required her full attention, and yet, her thoughts kept wandering.

What had her grandmother been trying to tell her with this pattern?

After several rows, Lizzie set the piece down and held it up to the light. The geometric design was beginning to take shape, but it was unlike anything her grandmother had ever made before. She had been known for her intricate doilies and delicate lace patterns, but this Afghan carried a boldness that felt out of place. The repeating shapes tugged at Lizzie's memory, though she couldn't quite place where she'd seen them before.

Her eyes moved back to the pattern. The handwriting was undeniably not her grandmother's, but some of the abbreviations and symbols weren't typical of anything Lizzie had seen in their shop's collection of books and guides. She ran her finger over the smooth paper, as though touching the words might unlock their meaning.

"Where have I seen this before?" she murmured to herself, leaning back against the sofa. *I'm certain the same pattern was on the counter of the shop in Erie,* she thought.

The frustration built as her mind replayed every glance at her grandmother's belongings, every journal entry she'd read, every conversation they'd had. It was all just out of reach, like trying to remember a dream slipping through her fingers.

Lizzie sighed, setting the unfinished Afghan aside. She rubbed her temples, the beginning of a headache pressing against her skull. "What were you trying to say, *Grossmommi?*" she whispered to the room, her voice breaking.

Just as she leaned forward to gather her materials and put them away, a knock sounded at the door, startling her. She froze, her heart leaping into her throat. Few people came by after dark, and for a moment, she debated whether to answer.

The knock came again, more insistent this time. Lizzie rose from the sofa, clutching the Afghan to her chest, and moved cautiously toward the door. Her hand hovered over the handle for a moment before she pulled it open.

Evert stood on the other side, his broad frame silhouetted against the faint moonlight. His expression was serious, his brow furrowed as though something weighed heavily on his mind. In his hand, he held a small envelope.

"I didn't mean to disturb you. But I found it in one of the boxes I took to sort through. I think you should see."

Lizzie blinked, momentarily caught off guard by his presence. She stepped aside, letting him in without a word. As he moved past her, she couldn't help but notice the tension in his shoulders and the way he clutched the envelope like it held the answer to everything.

"What is it?" she asked, closing the door behind him.

Evert handed her the envelope without meeting her gaze. "It's another note from your grandmother. I found it tucked in one of her old books."

Lizzie stared at the paper. The words were short but carried a weight that made her knees weak.

"*Look closer at what's hidden in plain sight*," Lizzie read aloud, her words hardly stirred the air. "*The truth is in the stitches.*"

Lizzie held the letter up to the light and then picked up the pattern. "Look at this," she whispered. "It's the same handwriting. There's no doubt whoever wrote this pattern sent my grandmother this note." Her eyes darted to the abandoned Afghan on the sofa. Evert followed her gaze, his expression sharpening.

"You've been working on that for days."

Lizzie nodded slowly. "I thought it was just another project, but now I'm not so sure."

Evert moved to the sofa and picked up the Afghan, studying the emerging pattern. His eyes narrowed as he turned it this way and that, then set it back down. "Do you think this is some kind of message?"

Lizzie nodded, the realization finally sinking in. "I don't

know why my grandmother was working on something like this."

Evert's gaze lingered on the project. "Whatever she was revealing, someone else might be trying to keep buried."

***

The sharp scent of fresh coffee mingled with the faint whiff of yarn dye that always seemed to linger in the back office of *Specialty Yarn and Goods*. Miriam sat in her chair, her fingers trembling as she unfolded the letter she had received a few weeks earlier that had managed to wedge itself between two unread sale catalogs. Her heart pounded as she recognized Esther's familiar handwriting.

Miriam,

You must tread carefully. I've done everything I can to shield the past, but the truth has a way of surfacing, and too many things are happening that may reveal your secret sooner than you hoped.

Esther

Esther's words struck a deep chord in Miriam's chest, the guilt she had long buried rushing to the surface. She pressed the letter to her lips for a brief moment before folding it tightly and tucking it into her apron pocket. The edges of the paper scratched her fingertips as if the message itself were chastising her for all the years of secrets and lies.

Her gaze drifted to the window, where the pale light of early evening added shadows across the walls. The shop was quiet now, Thomas having stepped into the stockroom to check inventory. Miriam's mind raced back to Esther's unyielding loyalty over the years. Despite the unbearable shame of her past, Esther had stood by her, holding her secrets as if they were her own.

The faint sound of footsteps brought Miriam back to the present. She abruptly turned and shoved the letter deeper into her pocket just as Thomas entered the room. His eyes narrowed as he noticed the unfinished Afghan spread across her lap.

"Still working on that?" he asked, his tone laced with suspicion.

Miriam nodded, keeping her expression unreadable. "It's a special project. A design someone shared with me recently."

Thomas grunted, leaning against the doorframe. "Seems like a waste of time now, don't you think? With everything else going on?"

Miriam kept her hands busy, tugging at the yarn and hooking a few stitches to maintain the illusion of nonchalance. "Sometimes, it's the small things that bring a little peace."

Thomas's brow furrowed, but he let the subject drop, retreating into the stockroom once more. Miriam exhaled a shaky breath, her thoughts swirling as she stared down at the pattern. The geometric design was almost complete, and though she hadn't admitted it to Thomas, the Afghan wasn't just a design that had mysteriously shown up in the mail one day.

Her fingers stilled as her mind wandered to the child she had left behind all those years ago. A pang of longing pierced her heart. Esther had been the bridge between Miriam and the boy. The money she'd sent, diligently funneled into a separate account, had been her way of assuring her that the child was well cared for.

Miriam had no right to feel regret now. She had chosen this life with Thomas, chosen to leave behind the past and the shame it carried. But Esther's letter reminded her that the past was never truly buried. Her friend's cryptic words tugged at Miriam's conscience, the significance of their meaning pressing heavy on her chest.

A faint rustling sound startled her. She looked up to see

Thomas returning, his sharp eyes scanning her face. "What's wrong with you tonight? You're acting jumpy."

Miriam forced a weak smile. "Just tired, that's all."

Thomas snorted. "We don't have time to be tired. There's too much at stake."

As he disappeared into the back again, Miriam reached into her pocket and withdrew the letter one final time. She read it over, committing Esther's words to memory before crumpling it into a ball and tossing it into the trash. "Oh, Evert," she whispered. "I pray you never find out the extent of our past sins. It's one thing for you to think we abandoned you; it's another to discover your parents have stolen what is rightfully yours."

***

The buggy rocked gently as it rolled along the dirt road, the crisp autumn air carrying the faint scent of fallen leaves and distant wood smoke. Evert held the reins with an ease he hadn't expected, the feel of the leather straps somehow familiar and foreign all at once. He glanced sideways at Lizzie, her face calm but reflective, her hands folded neatly in her lap.

"I still can't believe you talked me into this," he replied with a lopsided grin. "You're the first person to get me into a buggy in over a decade."

Lizzie glanced at him, her lips curving into a small smile. "Maybe it's not me. Maybe it's *Gott* reminding you where you came from."

He let the reins slide a bit, allowing the horse to slow as they approached a bend in the road. "Where I came from, huh?" He chuckled lightly, but there was no humor in it. "That's the problem. I'm not even sure where that is anymore."

Lizzie tilted her head, her voice steady. "I think you know more than you let on. You're just afraid to admit it."

Evert sighed, his gaze fixed on the horizon. "It's not just about finding out who my parents are. It's about... why they left."

Lizzie's heart ached at the raw vulnerability in his voice. "Have you ever thought that maybe *Gott* placed you where He wanted you to be? That He has a plan for your life, even if you don't understand it yet?"

Evert glanced at her, his brow furrowed. "You really believe that? That everything: being abandoned, leaving the Amish, all the mistakes I've made… was part of some grand plan?"

Lizzie nodded, her expression earnest. "I do. You can't keep running from the life He's calling you to live."

Her words struck a chord deep within him, stirring a longing he hadn't allowed himself to feel in years. He was quiet for a moment, his grip tightening on the reins as the buggy turned onto the main road leading into town.

He turned to her, his eyes searching hers. "You know, I didn't think much about coming back to Willow Springs until I met you. You make me feel like... like maybe there's something worth coming back for."

Lizzie's cheeks flushed, but her voice was firm. "Don't come back for me. Come back because you want to follow *Gott's* will. If you don't trust Him to guide your steps, you'll never find peace."

Evert's gaze lingered on her, a flicker of hope and longing in his expression. "Maybe you're right. Maybe it's time I stop running."

A few minutes later, they passed by Amos Zook's office, and Evert slowed the buggy. His eyes narrowed as they caught sight of the logo painted on the window, a series of interlocking geometric shapes. He leaned forward, his pulse quickening.

"Look at that."

Lizzie followed his gaze, her breath catching. "That

pattern... it's just like the one on the crochet project I'm working on."

Evert pulled the buggy to the side of the road as they both stared at the design on Amos's shop window. "Sure looks like the same design."

"It is. I'm sure of it. But why?" Lizzie asked.

***

The sharp clang of a dropped jar echoed through Jacob's herb shop as Ella scrambled to pick it up, her hands trembling. She carefully placed the jar back on the shelf, but it was too late to escape Jacob's notice. His face darkened as he turned from the counter, holding a small bundle of mislabeled herbs.

"Ella," he barked, his voice tight with frustration, "do you realize what this could have done? If someone used the wrong herb in their tea, it could hurt them. Or worse."

Tears welled up in Ella's eyes, her fingers fumbling with the hem of her apron. "I'm sorry, I didn't mean to mix them up."

Jacob slammed the mislabeled bundle on the counter, running a hand through his graying hair. "Sorry won't fix what could happen if this keeps up! You need to be more careful, Ella. We can't afford mistakes like this."

Ella held her breath, and the dam of guilt she'd been holding back irreversibly broke. "I think I already did... I think I made a mistake with Esther's order."

Jacob froze, his eyes narrowing. "What are you talking about?"

Ella clutched the edge of the counter, her voice trembling. "The day Esther came in... I might have mixed up the herbs. I didn't mean to, but I think... I think I gave her the wrong combination."

Jacob's face hardened as her words sank in. "Ella, do you realize what you're saying?"

Tears streamed down Ella's cheeks as she nodded. "I didn't mean to, Uncle Jacob! I was distracted, and I didn't double-check. What if I hurt her? What if it's my fault?"

Jacob's expression softened as he saw the genuine anguish in her eyes. He sighed noisily. "Listen to me. We don't know for sure that your mistake had anything to do with Esther's death. And even if it did, we can't let anyone find out. Do you understand me?"

Ella sniffled, her voice fragile as a thread "But what if... "

"*Nee*," Jacob interrupted firmly. "No 'what ifs.' This shop is all we have, Ella. If word gets out about this, our reputation will be ruined. I'll lose everything, and so will you."

Ella stared at him, her lips trembling. "But I can't live with this guilt, I feel like it's eating me alive."

Jacob squeezed her shoulder, his tone softening. "You'll learn to live with it, Ella. You have to. If you don't, you'll be forced to go back to Wisconsin, and you know what that means."

The mention of Wisconsin made Ella flinch. She closed her eyes, her breath coming in shallow gasps. "I can't go back there. I can't."

"Then you'll keep quiet," Jacob said, his voice unwavering. "We'll move forward, and we'll make sure nothing like this happens again. Do you understand?"

Ella nodded reluctantly, wiping her tears with the back of her sleeve. Jacob released her shoulder and turned back to the counter, his own hands trembling as he sorted through the herbs.

As Ella returned to her task, the guilt still churned in her stomach, but the fear of losing everything kept her silent. For now at least.

Tracy Fredrychowski

CHAPTER 11

Lizzie stood in the middle of the spare room, hands on her hips, surveying the chaos of half-sorted boxes, stacks of old books, and dusty knickknacks. Evert, already elbow-deep in a box marked "Winter Projects," held up a faded, half-knitted scarf.

"*Ach*, your grandmother had a knack for starting projects and never finishing them," he teased, waving the scarf like a flag. "Maybe it runs in the family?"

Lizzie shot him a playful glare. "Careful, or I'll add this to your pile of unfinished business."

Evert chuckled and folded the scarf tidily before tossing it into the donation pile. "Fair enough. But at least I can admit I'm a work in progress."

Lizzie smirked, pulling a dusty quilt from another box. "Aren't we all?"

As they worked, the rhythm of sorting through the clutter

turned into an almost comfortable routine. Evert's occasional jokes and Lizzie's exasperated comments filled the air, lightening the mood in what could have been a somber task.

Evert suddenly pulled out a rusted tin box with a latch. "What's this?" he asked, holding it up to Lizzie.

Lizzie peered over, brushing her hands off on her apron. "That's... I don't know. I don't think I've ever seen it before."

Evert popped the latch open, revealing a stack of old postcards and letters. "Looks like she kept everything. Even this one," he held up a postcard of Niagara Falls. "Who sends a postcard to someone who doesn't even travel?"

"*Grossmommi* had her ways," Lizzie said with a shrug. She glanced down at her pile and froze, her fingers brushing against an envelope that had slipped between two old pattern books. "What's that?" Evert asked, noticing her hesitation.

Lizzie didn't answer immediately. She cautiously unfolded the letter, her breath catching as she scanned the words. Her heart raced with each line.

The letter, written in Esther's perfect penmanship, was addressed to the church elders. It began innocently enough, mentioning some community concerns, but as Lizzie read further, the tone shifted.

Evert's curiosity got the better of him. "Lizzie? What does it say?"

Her voice was hardly audible as she read aloud: "*I can no longer keep silent. Amos Zook, has been defrauding the community for years under the guise of honest business. Jacob Stutzman has been coerced into cooperating, though I believe he's as much a victim as anyone else.*"

Evert let out a low whistle. "Well, that's... a lot."

Lizzie's hands trembled as she clutched the letter. "She knew. She knew all along. And she must have been trying to protect Jacob."

Evert stepped closer, his brow furrowed in concern. "Lizzie, this means your grandmother wasn't just caught in the middle of something small. She was trying to expose something big. No wonder she was... "

Lizzie cut him off, her voice tight with emotion. "You mean no wonder she was killed? That's what you were going to say, wasn't it?"

Evert hesitated, then nodded deliberately. "I don't want to jump to conclusions, but this letter... it's dangerous."

Lizzie sank onto the edge of an old trunk, staring at the letter in her hands. "Why didn't she tell me? Why didn't she trust me enough to warn me?"

Evert crouched beside her, his voice steady. "Maybe she thought the less you knew, the safer you'd be. But now we know. And we can't ignore this."

Lizzie nodded, wiping a tear from her cheek. "I just... I don't know where to start. And Jacob, what if he really didn't have a choice? I think we need to start with Jacob."

***

Lizzie stood at the counter of *Simply Yarn*, checking in on Ella before she went to speak to her uncle. The girl was busy sorting yarn skeins into neat rows, her hands moving with nervous energy that Lizzie couldn't ignore. Lizzie hesitated, then placed a reassuring hand on Ella's shoulder.

"I'm going to run an errand for a little while," Lizzie said, her tone casual. "I want to ensure you've got enough to keep you busy here."

Ella nodded hastily but avoided Lizzie's gaze. "*Jah*, I'll finish restocking this shelf and start organizing the new shipment."

Lizzie smiled, though her thoughts lingered on Ella's

anxious demeanor. "*Goot.*"

As Lizzie stepped outside, Evert was waiting for her, leaning against the front porch railing with his arms crossed.

"She okay?" Evert asked, nodding toward the shop.

"She's fine," Lizzie replied, picking up her grandmother's crochet bag from under the counter. "I just don't want her overhearing what we're about to discuss."

Evert raised an eyebrow but didn't press further. Together, they walked next door to the herb shop. The familiar chime of the bell above the door announced their arrival.

Jacob looked up from his counter, his face tightening the moment he saw them. His hands froze over a ledger he had been poring over, and his usual gruff demeanor faltered.

"Lizzie, Evert?"

Lizzie didn't waste time with pleasantries. "We need to talk, Jacob. Privately."

Jacob's eyes darted around the shop before he flipped the *Closed* sign over and locked the door. The air was thick with the scent of dried herbs, and Lizzie felt the moment pressing down on her as they stepped in closer.

Jacob's shoulders slumped. "What is this about?"

Evert folded his arms, his piercing gaze locking on Jacob.

"We've been piecing together some things. Things about Amos. About what he's been doing. And your name keeps coming up."

Jacob stiffened as he stepped behind the counter.

"We found a letter my grandmother wrote to the church elders. She knew what Amos was up to. She knew he was exploiting people. And she knew about your debts."

Jacob's face paled, and he sank into a chair. For a moment, the only sound was the faint rustle of leaves outside the window.

"She was trying to protect you, wasn't she?" Lizzie pressed. "That's why she got involved with Amos in the first place."

Jacob buried his face in his hands, his voice breaking as he spoke. "*Ach*, I didn't mean for any of this to happen. I was desperate. The herb shop was failing. Amos came to me with a deal, promised me he could help me turn things around. But it wasn't long before I realized what kind of man he really was."

Evert leaned forward, his tone firm. "What kind of deal?"

Jacob hesitated, then looked up, his eyes filled with shame. "Amos offered me a loan to keep the shop afloat, but the terms were impossible to meet. When I fell behind, he started threatening me, saying he'd ruin me if I didn't do as he said. He made me sell mislabeled herbs, fake remedies to the English, things I knew weren't right. But I didn't have a choice."

Lizzie's stomach churned. "And my grandmother? How did she get involved?"

Jacob's voice cracked as he continued. "Esther found out. She came to me and said she knew Amos was exploiting me. She tried to help, but Amos got wind of it. He started threatening her, too, saying he'd expose things she didn't want to come to light. I begged her to stay out of it, but you know your grandmother, she wouldn't back down."

Evert's jaw tightened. "And now she's gone. You think that's a coincidence?"

Jacob flinched, guilt etched into every line of his face. "I don't know. I don't want to think Amos had anything to do with it, but... I can't be sure."

"You should have told someone." Lizzie pleaded. "Maybe we could have done something."

Jacob shook his head, tears brimming in his eyes. "I didn't want you to get hurt, and I didn't want anyone else to get dragged into this mess."

Evert stepped closer, his voice thick with emotion. "Amos needs to be stopped. But we need your help. We need everything you know about him."

Jacob hesitated, then nodded sluggishly. "I'll do what I can.

But you need to be careful. Amos... he's not a man to cross."

The tension in Jacob's shop was deep as Jacob sat slumped at the counter, his hands gripping the edges of a ledger that he hadn't opened in weeks, his face etched with worry.

"Jacob," Lizzie began mildly, her voice steady but firm. "You know my grandmother wouldn't have wanted any of this to continue. If we don't act, Amos will just keep hurting people for his own gain. She tried to protect you, to shield you from him. But now, we need your help."

Jacob looked up at Lizzie, his eyes weary and rimmed with guilt. "I know what you're asking, but you don't understand what's at stake. Amos doesn't just make threats; he follows through. If I go to the elders, he'll drag me down with him, and he'll destroy Ella too."

Evert, leaning against the counter with his arms crossed, interjected. "Do you think Amos is going to stop just because you stay quiet? He'll find another way to manipulate you or someone else. It's what he does. The only way to end this is to expose him. If you don't, he's going to ruin more lives; yours, Ella's, and whoever else he decides to target."

Jacob's hand trembled as he rubbed his temples. "You don't understand. I owe Amos more than just money. He has enough dirt on me to ruin everything I've built here. My reputation, my business... gone in an instant. And Ella..." His voice cracked as he trailed off.

Lizzie leaned forward, placing a hand on the table. "Jacob, I know you're scared. We all are. But *Grossmommi* believed in you. She believed you were better than this, that you could stand up to him. Why else would she try so hard to protect you? If you don't speak out, everything she worked for will have been in vain."

Jacob stared down at the ledger, his thoughts visibly racing. "Esther..." he muttered, shaking his head. "She was always trying to help, even when I didn't deserve it. She begged me to walk away from Amos's schemes, but I was in too deep. I didn't listen."

"Then listen now," Evert said, his tone softer but no less insistent. "This is your chance to make things right. To honor her memory and protect Ella from whatever Amos has planned next. He's counting on your silence. Don't give him that power."

Jacob's shoulders sagged under the weight of their words. He opened the ledger in front of him, flipping through its pages with a resigned sigh. "If I do this," he uttered, "it'll cost me everything."

Lizzie exchanged a glance with Evert before speaking. "If we work together, we can make sure it costs Amos more. We can prove he's the one behind all this. But we can't do it without you."

Jacob looked at Lizzie, then Evert, his eyes clouded with fear and guilt. He nodded. "Alright, I'll talk to the elders."

Lizzie and Evert nodded; their determination renewed. The three of them sat together, laying out a plan to gather the evidence needed to present to the church elders.

As they wrote out their plan, Lizzie suddenly remembered where she had seen the perfect penmanship found in both the crochet pattern and the note. It was Jacob's.

"You sent a warning note to my grandmother, and it was you who gave her the Afghan pattern she was working on, wasn't it?" Lizzie asked.

Evert folded his arms, his voice low but curious. "Why that pattern? Why embed Amos's logo?

Jacob laid his pen aside and cradled his face in his hands. "Because I couldn't go public," he said. "Not without dragging your families, and mine, through the muck. But I knew Amos was up to no good. The fake merchandise, the blackmail, the pressure he put on desperate men like me... I saw too much, and I said too little." He paused before continuing. "I couldn't stop him. But I could plant the seed. So, I reached out to two women who knew how to make threads tell a story."

Lizzie sighed. "*Grossmommi* and Miriam Mast?"

Jacob nodded. "Esther saw through Amos from the beginning. I needed to leave a trail; quiet, hidden, but there if she needed it.

Evert leaned forward. "And Miriam?"

Jacob hesitated before answering. "She had regrets. Being tied to Amos... it cost her more than anyone knows."

Lizzie pulled out the project from the bag and looked down at the pattern again, her fingers brushing the familiar shapes that now held so much more meaning.

"You were trying to warn her," she whispered. "All along." Jacob gave a quiet nod. "I needed someone to know the truth if anything happened to me. I didn't expect someone to get to Esther first... I really thought it would be me."

***

Amos stood silently in the doorway of the vacant building

across from Jacob's herb shop, his wide-brimmed hat pulled low over his face. The air was crisp, with the scent of fallen leaves lingering in the breeze, but Amos barely noticed. His sharp eyes were fixed on the small shop across the street.

He had been on his way to confront Jacob when he saw them. Lizzie Yoder, with her determined stride, followed closely by Evert Miller, the thorn in his side that refused to disappear. Amos narrowed his eyes as he watched them step into Jacob's shop. Moments later, the *Closed* sign appeared in the window, and Amos's jaw clenched.

He grumbled under his breath, his fingers twitching at his sides. "Jacob better be figuring out how to get rid of them for good."

Amos shifted vaguely, ensuring he stayed hidden in the doorway's shadow. His patience was wearing thin, and the sight of Lizzie and Evert together in that shop only fueled his growing irritation. Jacob was under his thumb, obedient and pliable, and he didn't need those two stirring up trouble and planting seeds of doubt in his well-laid-out plans.

He muttered to himself, "The old man better remember where his loyalties lie."

As he waited, Amos's thoughts churned. The mere sight of

Evert Miller was enough to set his teeth on edge. The boy was supposed to be gone, far from Willow Springs, far from the past Amos had worked so hard to bury. Instead, he'd returned, sniffing around and asking questions he had no business asking. Amos chuckled darkly to himself. "Just like his father, always pushing where he shouldn't. He couldn't chance the discovery before he had a chance to cover all his tracks once and for all."

He adjusted his hat and propped against the doorframe, his mind racing. He couldn't let them derail his plans. Jacob had been a loyal, if reluctant, pawn in his schemes, but if the man started to waver, Amos wouldn't hesitate to remind him of the consequences. And if Lizzie and Evert got too close to the truth…

Amos's lips curled into a sneer. He wouldn't let it come to that. He had spent years crafting his network of suppliers, his deftly curated façade, and his position in the community. Esther Yoder had already complicated things with her threats, but her sudden death had silenced her for good. Now, it seemed her granddaughter and that meddlesome Evert were picking up where she left off.

The shop door opened suddenly, and Amos tensed, slipping further into the shadows. He watched as Lizzie and Evert stepped out, their faces serious. They exchanged a few words on the sidewalk before heading off down the street, their pace brisk. Amos didn't move, his eyes following them until they disappeared around the corner.

Only then did he step out of the doorway, his boots scraping against the pavement as he crossed the street toward the herb shop. His patience had run out.

Jacob would answer to him. And if the old man had any ideas about switching sides, Amos would make sure he understood the cost.

* * *

Ella pushed open the herb shop's back door quietly, the hinges' familiar creak echoing ever so lightly in the wind. She slipped inside, the comforting scent of dried herbs and freshly brewed tea welcoming her. She set her shawl on the hook by the door and reached for her lunch basket, ready to join her uncle for their midday meal. But as she stepped toward the kitchen, voices stopped her in her tracks.

"You've been dragging your feet," Amos's gruff voice cut through the quiet of the shop, sharp and accusatory. "I'm done waiting for you to handle this."

Ella froze, her breath catching in her throat. She pressed herself against the wall, hidden from view, her heart pounding as she listened.

"I told you…" Jacob said, his voice strained with frustration. "I'm doing everything I can. But you know I'm not the kind of man to… "

"To what?" Amos interrupted, his tone dripping with disdain. "I've been patient, but my patience is wearing thin."

There was a long pause, and Ella could hear her uncle's heavy sigh. She could picture him rubbing his temples like he always did when stressed.

"Maybe it's time someone knows exactly where Ella's been hiding. I'm sure he'd be very interested to find out where his wayward bride-to-be ran off to."

Ella's hand flew to her mouth, stifling a gasp. Her knees threatened to buckle as the pressure of Amos's words sank in. She clutched the edge of the counter to steady herself, her mind racing. How did Amos know? She had done everything in her power to keep her past in Wisconsin hidden. Even Jacob didn't know the full extent of her reasons for leaving until much later. And now Amos threatened to destroy the fragile peace she had built in Willow Springs.

"I'm warning you, Amos," Jacob said, his voice trembling with suppressed anger. "If you so much as think about contacting Hostetler, you'll regret it. Ella's my family. I won't let you ruin her."

"Regret it?" Amos sneered. "Don't make me laugh. You're in no position to make threats. Not with the mountain of debt you owe me. Not with the fake invoices I've been so generously overlooking for you. Face it... you're mine to command. And if you don't want me dragging your niece's name through the mud, you'll do as I say."

Ella felt tears prick at her eyes as she listened to Amos's venomous words. She wanted to storm into the room, to scream at Amos to leave them alone, but fear rooted her to the spot. If Amos had the power to send her back to Wisconsin, to Ura, then she had to tread carefully.

"I'll take care of it, but leave Ella out of this. She's got nothing to do with any of it."

"See that she doesn't," Amos said coldly. "And Jacob... don't make me come back here again. Next time, it won't just be words."

Ella heard heavy footsteps heading toward the back door, and she ducked into the pantry, scarcely breathing as Amos strode past. When the door slammed shut, she braced against the shelves, trembling, her mind a whirlwind of fear and dread.

Ella stepped out of the pantry, her thoughts swirling. What had she done to bring undue worry to her sweet uncle? Guilt pressed powerfully on her chest as she stepped back outside to reenter, making her presence known to her uncle.

Maybe it was time she returned to Wisconsin and faced what she'd been running from. Only then would Amos lose his leverage over her uncle. But the thought of confronting Ura sent a chill through her.

She turned to step back into the shop, but before she could open the door, a hand clamped firmly over her mouth, and an arm gripped her like a vise, covering her in fear.

Her muffled cry was silenced by the cold, low voice in her ear. "Got you, my little insurance policy," the voice hissed, his tone sharp and full of malice.

Tracy Fredrychowski

CHAPTER 12

L izzie poured two cups of coffee, the comforting aroma filling her tiny kitchen. She handed one to Evert, who was sitting at the small table, absently fiddling with his straw hat.

She settled against the counter, eyeing him with a playful smile. "Well, look at you," she teased, nodding at the hat. "A straw hat with jeans and a T-shirt, you're going to confuse people."

Evert chuckled, sliding the hat onto his head and tipping it dramatically. "Think I could start a new trend?"

Lizzie laughed, shaking her head. "Admittedly, it fits you better than that ball cap you're always wearing. But it's a little strange seeing you in it. Do you feel at home in it?"

He turned the hat in his hands, his expression softening. "Actually... yeah. It does feel right. Strange, huh? Like it pulls at something deep, even though I've been gone so long."

Lizzie tilted her head, studying him. "Do you miss it? The

Amish life, I mean."

Evert took a sip of his coffee, the question clearly making him pause. He let out a small sigh. "I miss the community, the way people look out for each other. The simplicity of it all. But then I think about how much I enjoy my truck, my freedom to come and go as I please. It would take something, or someone, pretty special to make me give all that up."

Lizzie arched a brow, her tone light but pointed. "That sounds a lot like the kind of decision *Gott* should put on your heart, don't you think? Not just a person."

Evert grinned, leaning back in his chair.

"I think it's more about reminding you that you can't outrun what *Gott* has planned for you," she said tenderly. "It's not about the truck or the freedom. It's about trusting Him to show you where you belong."

Evert looked at her, the teasing in his eyes replaced with something softer. "Maybe you're right. Guess I've been running so long, I didn't even realize I was tired."

Lizzie smiled warmly. "Sometimes it's not about running at all. It's about standing still long enough to listen."

Evert tipped his hat toward her. "You should write that down. Pretty wise for someone who spends most of her time surrounded by yarn."

Lizzie laughed, but the sincerity in her voice lingered. "You'll figure out where you belong at some point."

He nodded thoughtfully, sipping his coffee in silence. For the first time in a long time, she felt he had the faintest pull toward something more settled.

The soft clink of Evert setting his coffee cup on the table broke the quiet rhythm of their conversation. Evert leaned forward, resting his elbows on the table, the straw hat now perched on the edge, forgotten for the moment.

"I keep thinking about that note your grandmother wrote," Evert began, his brow furrowing. "The one she planned to send to the bishop. It ties so many things together, but not enough to make it clear. Amos... Jacob. They're tangled up in something bigger."

Lizzie nodded, her fingers brushing the edge of the table. "*Grossmommi* knew something she wasn't supposed to, and it cost her. Jacob's involvement; it's obvious but he's trying to make things right. Still, he's only one piece of the puzzle."

Evert exhaled, his jaw tightening. "Jacob's confession gave us more questions than answers. And Esther's warning..." He rubbed a hand over his face. "I feel like I need to talk to those two from the shop in Erie again. I think they're involved in this more than they let on."

Lizzie glanced at him, hesitating. "You think they'll tell you anything more?"

Evert shrugged. "I don't know, but I have to try. Something about the way they acted last time... it felt off. And now, knowing what we do about Amos's schemes and how they might have been involved..." His voice trailed off, and he looked at Lizzie, his expression earnest. "I'm going to Erie. Would you want to ride along?"

Lizzie shook her head. "I can't; I need to get back to the shop. I've already taken a longer lunch than normal. Besides, I don't think they'd open up to me any more than they would to you."

Evert nodded, reaching for his hat. "I've dealt with folks like them before... ones who think they can hide everything behind a polite smile and a locked door."

As he turned to leave, Lizzie lingered for a moment until the door closed behind him. She felt a pang of unease. Something about Evert heading to Erie alone didn't sit right, but she pushed the thought aside, confident he could handle whatever lay ahead, at least, she hoped so.

***

The little bell above the back door jingled as Lizzie unlocked and pushed it open, stepping into the familiar scent of yarn. The morning sun had long since passed its peak, and the afternoon light filtered in through the windows, highlighting the tidy rows of skeins. Everything was as she'd left it that morning; except for one thing.

The shop was still closed.

Lizzie frowned, her eyes immediately catching the '*Gone to Lunch*' sign hanging in the window. Shaking her head, Lizzie moved to flip the sign and unlock the door, welcoming in the few customers already waiting outside.

As the day unfolded, Lizzie busied herself with restocking shelves, answering questions, and helping a steady stream of customers. Yet through the hum of activity, a nagging thought kept surfacing: Ella hadn't shown up. Lizzie glanced at the clock. Ella's lunch break should have ended nearly an hour ago.

The door opened again, and Lizzie looked up to see Jacob stepping inside, a brown paper sack in hand. His face was lined with worry as he glanced around the shop.

"I thought I'd bring Ella's lunch over," he said, holding up the sack. "Figured she must've been too busy to join me today."

Lizzie froze mid-step, her heart dropping. "Jacob, I haven't seen Ella since this morning. She hasn't gotten back from lunch yet."

Jacob's brows furrowed, his hand tightening around the bag. "That's strange."

Lizzie set down the skeins of yarn she was sorting, her concern deepening. "She must've run an errand she forgot to mention. But she didn't say anything to me about it earlier."

Jacob glanced at the clock on the wall, his expression growing more troubled. "She's not one to wander off without telling someone. It's not like her."

Lizzie bit her lip, trying to suppress the rising tide of worry. "Did she seem... upset or distracted this morning? Maybe something's bothering her."

Jacob hesitated, his jaw tightening before he shook his head. "She was quiet, but that's nothing new. I don't know," he admitted, setting the lunch sack on the counter. "But I'll go check around town, see if anyone's seen her. She can't have gone far."

Lizzie nodded, trying to stay calm for both their sakes. "I'll keep an eye out here, and I'll ask the customers if they've seen her. Let me know if you find anything."

As Jacob turned to leave, Lizzie caught sight of the paper sack he'd left behind. It sat there, untouched, a glaring reminder of Ella's absence. A prickle of unease crept up her spine. Ella's disappearance was beginning to feel less like an oversight and more like something far more unsettling.

***

Evert's truck idled momentarily before he shut off the engine, and gripped the steering wheel securely. From his vantage point in the parking lot, he watched Miriam and Thomas through the shop window. Miriam stood behind the counter, chatting with a customer, her movements deliberate and precise. Thomas worked near the back, arranging a display of spools and yarn, his posture rigid and controlled.

Something about Miriam struck a chord deep in his chest. Her mannerisms... the tilt of her head as she listened, the subtle way she tapped her fingers against the counter, reminded him of his grandmother. His pulse quickened. The sinking feeling he'd experienced during his last visit returned with a vengeance, gnawing at him. He couldn't ignore it any longer.

He leaned back in his seat, staring at the couple. His mind churned with memories and half-formed connections. Could it really be? Could Miriam and Thomas be the parents he'd spent years searching for, the ones his grandmother had protected him from?

Evert inhaled deeply. Once the last customer exited the shop, he stepped out of his truck and strode to the door. When he pushed it open, Miriam's head shot up, her warm smile faltering when she recognized him.

Evert closed the door and, without a word, locked it. The click echoed in the small shop. He pulled the shades down on the door's glass window, blocking out the view from the street.

"What's the meaning of this?" Thomas demanded, his tone sharp and accusatory.

Evert ignored him, turning to Miriam. "I've been looking for answers my whole life."

Miriam's face paled, her hand trembling as she clutched the edge of the counter. "You should leave," Thomas snapped, stepping forward.

"I'm not going anywhere," Evert shot back, his rebellious streak flashing to the surface. He stood his ground, glaring at the older man. "Not until you tell me the truth."

"We already told you," Thomas said, his voice rising. "We don't know anything about your so-called parents."

Evert slammed his hand on the counter, the sound reverberating through the shop. "Don't lie to me! I know it's you. Nathan and Rebecca—those are your real names, aren't they? You're my parents."

Miriam gasped, her hand flying to her mouth. Thomas's jaw tightened, his face flushing red with anger.

"I deserve to know," Evert continued, his voice breaking a tad. "Why did you leave me? Why didn't you take me with you?"

Miriam's resolve crumbled. Tears streamed down her face as she collapsed onto a stool behind the counter. "Evert..." she whispered, her voice trembling. "We didn't have a choice."

"Miriam!" Thomas barked, his face contorted with rage. "Stop this nonsense."

Evert turned his glare on Thomas. "You've been running from this for years, haven't you? My grandparents protected me from whatever mess you made."

Thomas sneered. "You have no room to talk. We sent money to your grandmother to care for you, to hold it in escrow until you were old enough to use it. But only if you stayed Amish. That was the deal. And you failed."

Evert recoiled as if struck. "Failed?" he said, his voice rising. "I didn't even know who I was, let alone what deals you made behind my back."

"You didn't stay in the community," Thomas said coldly. "It's rightfully ours since you left your heritage behind."

"Don't talk to me about heritage. If that were so important, you wouldn't have walked away from yours." Evert took a few minutes to calm himself before continuing, "You don't care about me," Evert spat, his fists clenched at his sides. "You never did."

"Don't you dare judge us," Thomas snarled. "You don't know what we sacrificed."

Miriam sobbed quietly, shaking her head. "We thought we were doing what was best for you," she whispered. "But I've regretted it every day of my life."

Thomas rolled his eyes. "Regret won't pay the bills, Miriam. And it won't change the past. We only want what's rightfully ours."

"I have no idea what you're talking about. What was rightfully yours?" Evert spat.

Thomas quickly replied, "The money in the account. That's why you're here, right?"

Evert walked closer to his father. "The last thing I care about is money. All I care about is the truth." Evert's voice softened as he turned to Miriam. "If you regretted it so much, why didn't you ever come back for me?"

Miriam looked at him with tear-filled eyes. "Because we were cowards," she admitted. "And by the time we realized what we'd done, it was too late."

Evert swallowed the lump in his throat, his emotions warring within him. Anger, sadness, and a flicker of pity churned together.

"All I care about is finding out what happened to Esther, and you can bet if you both had something to do with her death, you'll have more than me to deal with."

"We have no idea what happened to Esther; her death was as much a shock to us as to everyone else," Thomas spat.

"Please, Evert, you have to believe we did what we thought was best for you. Your best hope for a normal life was living with your grandparents. We'd gotten ourselves too involved in things that could come back to haunt us… with people who knew more about us than we knew ourselves." Miriam paused to wipe her nose before continuing. "Esther was our only connection to you. She kept our secret, and we sent her money to give to your grandparents to raise you."

Thomas stepped between them. "You didn't keep your end of the bargain, so we took it back. All of it!" Thomas moved to unlock the door. "So, if you've come to collect, I'm afraid you're in for another big disappointment."

"Not that I care about the money, but why?"

"Because we needed it to get out from beneath our debts. To make a fresh start," his father replied.

Evert furrowed his brow, trying to understand, and then he had to ask. "Amos Zook?"

"We were so naïve. We didn't realize what we were doing before it was too late, and then we were in too deep." Miriam cried.

"I can't believe you're messed up in all of this," Evert said, throwing his arms into the air. "Zook must be stopped."

Thomas scoffed, but Evert ignored him, turning and walking out of the shop. All he could hear as he left was Miriam's quiet sobs and Thomas's muttered curses.

***

Evert stepped into the yarn shop just as Lizzie was flipping the *Closed* sign on the door. Lizzie glanced up, her face pale and lined with worry.

"You're back."

He opened his mouth to tell her about Erie, about Miriam and Thomas, but her troubled expression stopped him short. "What's wrong?"

"It's Ella," Lizzie said, pulling her sweater tighter around her middle. "She's gone."

Evert frowned, stepping closer. "Gone? What do you mean?"

Lizzie sighed. "She didn't come back from lunch and Jacob's been looking all over town. He thought maybe she ran an errand, but no one's seen her. I think... I think she ran away."

"Ran away?" Evert repeated, his voice sharp. "She wouldn't just run off without telling someone."

"She's been so quiet lately, something's been bothering her, I know it. But I thought if I gave her time, she'd tell me."

"We need to call the police."

"*Nee*," Lizzie said quickly, shaking her head. "It's not their place to get involved in our community."

"This isn't just an Amish matter. Ella could be in real

danger."

Lizzie hesitated, her worry etched deep. "I just… I don't know."

The tension hung heavily between them as Lizzie locked the shop and they walked back to her grandmother's cottage.

Inside the cottage, Lizzie lit a lamp over the table. "I just can't believe she'd leave without saying anything," she said softly, sinking into a chair.

Evert remained standing, his hands on his hips. "Amos is tied up in this mess with Miriam and Thomas. Esther knew about it, and it's all connected to his underhanded connections to the black market. He pulled Amos, Miriam, and Thomas into his business, and now they all feel trapped."

Lizzie leaned over the table. "But why would they trust Amos? He's a crook."

"Because he and my father were friends at one point, and he swindled them into believing his lies," Evert said, his voice bitter. He shook his head, his frustration boiling over.

"Your parents? Are you sure?"

"*Jah*. They admitted it, but I don't even know why I care."

"Because you care, and you care about finding the truth. About protecting what's right."

Her words hit him like a punch to the chest. Evert sank into a chair, running a hand over his face. "I don't know. Maybe knowing the truth isn't worth the trouble."

Lizzie sat beside him, her gaze steady. "You've been searching for answers, for family, all this time. That has to be worth something, and besides, you want to make it right, and that's commendable."

Evert looked at her, his eyes searching hers. For a moment, the air between them felt charged, unspoken emotions bubbling to the surface. "You have a lot of faith in me," he whispered.

"Someone has to," Lizzie said with a small smile.

They were both silent when a knock at the door interrupted their conversation. The door creaked open, and Jacob stepped in, his hat in his hands, worry etched deep in his features.

"Jacob," Lizzie said, her voice tinged with concern. "Did you find anything?"

Jacob hesitated, glancing at Evert before speaking. "I found this." He held up Ella's shawl, their soft blue fibers a stark contrast against his calloused fingers. "Hanging by the back door. I'm sure she had it on this morning when she left for the yarn shop."

Lizzie furrowed her brow. "Then why would it be there?"

"I don't know," Jacob admitted, his voice strained. "But Amos came to see me right after you two left the shop. I'm afraid... I'm afraid Ella overheard our conversation."

Evert leaned forward, his eyes narrowing. "What did Amos say?"

Jacob sighed heavily, sinking into a chair at the table. "He's threatened to send word to someone Ella is hiding from, telling him where to find her. He's using her past to keep me in line."

Lizzie exchanged a glance with Evert before turning back to Jacob. "What happened in Wisconsin? What is she running from?"

Jacob pulled on his long graying beard, the lines of his age deepening with the weight of his confession. "Ella was promised to the bishop's son. At first, it seemed like a good match. But she started to see things in him that... well, that no young woman should have to endure. He has a temper, a violent one, and a fondness for *Englisch* women. When Ella confronted him about his behavior, he didn't deny it. He told her she'd have no choice but to obey him once they were married, and she would need to lay a blind eye to his hobbies."

Lizzie's hand flew to her mouth. "Oh, Jacob."

"She begged her father to call off the engagement," Jacob

continued, his voice cracking. "But the bishop had already given his blessing, and her father didn't see a way out. So he sent her here, to me, hoping I could keep her safe until he could figure out a way out of her commitment."

Evert crossed his arms, his jaw tight. "And Amos knows about this?"

Jacob nodded miserably. "He's been holding it over my head for months. If word gets out, Ura Hostetler will come for her. She'll be sent back and forced to marry him, and I can't let that happen."

Lizzie sat down, her hands trembling. "Do you think she ran away, Jacob? Or do you think Amos...?"

Jacob looked at her, the anguish in his eyes unmistakable. "I don't know. But Amos wants me to do his bidding. He wants you gone, Evert, and for Lizzie to stop digging into Esther's affairs."

Evert's voice was cold, calculated. "He's trying to keep us all in line. He knows we're getting too close to his business."

Jacob nodded. "That's what I'm afraid of. If Amos thinks Ella could be used as leverage, he won't hesitate. And if she overheard us, she might've run off to keep him from using her against me."

As the strain of their conversation settled over them, the three sat in silence, their determination growing stronger with each passing moment.

CHAPTER 13

The stockroom was cold. The concrete floor beneath Ella's legs sent a steady chill through her bones, and the musty scent of damp cardboard boxes made her stomach turn. Her wrists ached from where they'd been roughly tied together behind her with thick twine, but the true discomfort came from the gnawing fear coiled in her gut.

She shifted, pressing her back against a wooden crate marked with faded, unreadable lettering. She took a long, deep breath as she tried to still her trembling fingers. She had to focus. Panicking wouldn't get her out of this.

Beyond the door, muffled voices filtered through, their tones sharp and urgent. Ella held her breath, straining to make out their words.

"...not leaving it up to chance."

"Evert Miller is getting too close."

Evert? Ella's pulse quickened. Why were they talking about

him?

A phone rang, the sudden shrill sound making her flinch. The conversation shifted. One voice gruff but familiar rose above the other. Amos.

"You listen to me," Amos snapped into the phone. "I didn't get this far just to have some self-righteous boy and that nosy shopkeeper ruin everything. He should've stayed gone. And now he's sniffing around with that girl, piecing things together like they got some *Gott*-given right to meddle in my affairs."

Ella shuddered. Lizzie. He was talking about Lizzie too. She swallowed hard, her mind racing. Whatever Evert and Lizzie had uncovered had made Amos desperate. Desperate men did dangerous things.

There was a pause, then Amos's voice dropped to a lethal growl.

"You forget, I know exactly what you've been up to. Every single shipment, every transaction. If I go down, you go down with me."

Ella closed her eyes, realization settling over her like a heavy blanket. Amos wasn't working alone. He had leverage over someone else, someone powerful enough to be afraid of exposure.

The illegal goods. The fake Amish-made merchandise. That was it. If word got out that Amos had been passing off imported products from China as genuine Amish craftsmanship, his entire business would crumble.

But that still didn't explain why she was here.

Her thoughts were interrupted by a second voice, rougher, angrier.

"We should just get rid of her. She knows too much."

Ella's heart slammed against her ribs. Her fingers curled into fists, and she swallowed back the rising fear. It wasn't Amos's voice that haunted her.

Why was he involved? How did he fit into all of this?

Her mind spun, trying to piece it together... what was his role?

Ella pressed her bound hands against the crate behind her, forcing herself to think. She couldn't afford to wait for someone to rescue her. She had to save herself.

Amos was smart, but he was also greedy. If she could convince them that she was useful, that she could get information from inside the yarn shop, maybe, just maybe, she could buy herself time.

She inhaled slowly, steadying her nerves.

***

The dim yellow light in Amos's office flickered as he settled back in his chair and reached for his pipe, tapping it against the ashtray on his desk, but before he could light it, the phone rang. The sharp, jarring tone cut through the quiet office, sending an instant spike of irritation through him.

He picked up the receiver with a rough, "What?" On the other end, a familiar voice responded, tight with frustration. Thomas Mast.

"Amos," Thomas said, his voice clipped. "We're done."

Amos stilled, gripping the receiver tightly. "What do you mean, done?"

"I mean," Thomas snapped, "Miriam and I are selling the shop. We're leaving Erie."

Amos's lips curled into a sneer. "You don't just walk away from this, Mast."

"You think I care?" Thomas shot back. "We never should have been mixed up in this mess to begin with."

Amos leaned forward, his voice a low growl. "You got what you needed because of me. Because I let you buy in to what I built. You think you can just run?"

"I don't care anymore," Thomas hissed. "Miriam and I have more to lose than you do. We were stupid to ever let you pull us into this, and now that boy, our son, is sniffing around. I won't risk my freedom or my wife's safety just because you want to keep playing your games."

"You're afraid of Evert?" Amos scoffed, shaking his head. "He's nothing more than a lost cause trying to piece together a past that doesn't exist anymore. He'll get tired of chasing ghosts and leave, just like he did before."

"Maybe," Thomas said. "Or maybe he won't stop until he figures everything out. And when he does, do you really think he won't find a way to take you down?"

Amos let out a dry chuckle. "Let him try."

The conversation continued for a few more minutes until Thomas stood his ground. "I'm telling you," Thomas pressed, his voice sharp, "we're done. We're not buying from you anymore, we're not taking your shipments, and we're not going to cover for you. You wanted us to keep Evert away from the truth? That's your problem now."

A slow, simmering anger rose in Amos's chest. "You really think you can just walk away from this without consequences?"

"I have to." Thomas sighed heavily, his words hanging between them. "For Miriam. For me. For what little future we have left."

Amos clenched his jaw, feeling the first real stirrings of panic. If Thomas and Miriam walked away, he lost more than two business partners and his strongest connections to the supply chain.

Amos let out a slow breath, trying to rein in his temper. "If you go now, don't expect me to clean up your mess."

The line went dead.

Amos stayed still for a long moment, the dial tone buzzing in his ear before he ultimately slammed the phone down onto the desk.

The heavy scent of dust clung to the air, mixing with the faint bitterness of toxic herbs Amos had been packaging for resale. It wasn't an elegant operation, but it was his. And he didn't let anyone, not the church elders, not the law, and certainly not some hotheaded fool from Wisconsin threaten it.

Ura Hostetler leaned against the doorframe, looking far too comfortable for a man who should be desperate. Amos had expected as much. The young man had the same air about him as every other snake he had dealt with over the years; a confidence that came from knowing all the wrong people.

"So, you got what I asked for?" Amos asked, shuffling a few invoices off his desk as he took a seat.

Ura smirked, pulling a small notebook from his pocket. He tossed it onto Amos's desk, the worn leather cover landing with a dull thud. "Everything you need. The right contacts. The right shipping routes. The right people who don't ask questions about where things come from. You'll have the kind of access you need."

Amos flipped through the pages, scanning the names, addresses, and details that would expand his business beyond the small Amish suppliers he had been using. These were *Englisch* contacts, real buyers who would pay top dollar for what he could sell them. Fake Amish-made goods, cheaply produced but sold at a premium to tourists who had no idea the difference between an authentic hand-woven quilt and something stitched together in a factory overseas.

"You do good work, Hostetler," Amos admitted. "Shame you didn't use those smarts to make an honest living."

Ura laughed, stepping closer and tossing the black spray paint can he had used a few days earlier in Amos' direction. "You and I both know there's no honest living that gets you ahead in this world."

Amos caught the can and then smirked, but didn't disagree.

Ura continued, his voice smooth. "You needed my connections, and I needed something in return. You did a little digging, checked in with some of your 'friends' and wouldn't you know it, Ella ran straight into your town trying to hide."

Amos chuckled darkly. "Didn't expect you to come all this way after her, though. You've been here for weeks. What took you so long to come claim what was yours?"

"I had some unfinished business to see to first, and I knew she wouldn't be going anywhere." Ura's expression darkened. "She was promised to me. And I don't let what's mine get away so easily. Being married will make a great cover for me among the *People*."

Amos leaned forward, resting his forearms on the desk. "Listen, Hostetler. You brought me information. I brought you Ella. That's the deal. Now, your job is to keep that little thing quiet. She may already know more than she ought to, and I'm expecting you to keep your future *fraa* under control."

***

Jacob paced the small back room of his herb shop, his hands shaking as he gripped the letter he had received from his *bruder* in Wisconsin, his words thick with concern and something that sent ice through Jacob's veins.

"The bishop was here this morning, and Ura told him he was on his way to bring Ella home."

Jacob gasped. His grip tightened on the paper as he continued to read.

"The bishop mentioned it in passing, like it was already decided. As if Ella had no say in the matter. Ura's got his mind set on bringing her back."

Jacob sank onto a stool, his mind racing. Ella was gone. Had Ura already found her and taken her against her will?

He swallowed hard. "If Ura got to her first, *Gott* help us." There was too much happening at once, too many unknowns. He stared blankly at the wall.

With a newfound sense of urgency, Jacob pulled out a ledger and forced himself to focus. There was an order to fill, and his hands needed something to do before his mind unraveled completely.

As he measured out dried herbs and placed them into carefully labeled pouches, his eyes landed on a crumpled sheet of paper near the back of his worktable. Frowning, he smoothed it out, recognizing Ella's handwriting.

It was a note... a list of herbs for Esther's last tea order. His heart pounded as he scanned the ingredients. Chamomile. Peppermint. Ginger.

Jacob's breath came in sharp and fast. Nothing toxic.

Jacob nearly knocked over a container of dried lavender, but as he turned, something nagged at him.

His gaze landed on the row of labeled herb jars; the very ones Ella had handled before Esther's last order. She had been so convinced she had made a mistake, but had she?

With a sharp inhale, he yanked the jars from the shelf, one by one. Suspiciously, he unscrewed the lids and took a deep whiff of each. Chamomile. Mint. Ginger.

The scents were distinct, familiar. Harmless.

Jacob's hands worked faster, moving down the line. There was nothing here that could have caused Esther's death. Not a single jar. Not a single mislabeled herb.

His heart pounded as he reached the last one. The one Ella had sworn she had mistaken. He lifted it to his nose and inhaled deeply. Nothing but dried lemongrass.

His fingers trembled as he clenched the jars and placed them back on the shelf.

It was never Ella.

It had never been the tea.

A wave of relief and horror crashed over him. She had been carrying guilt for something she never did. And worse, she might have run straight into danger because of it.

By the time he reached *Simply Yarn*, his chest was heaving. He found Lizzie near the counter, eyes wide with worry.

"Jacob?" Lizzie set down a basket of skeins. "Did you find her?"

"*Nee.*" Jacob raked a hand through his graying hair, catching his breath. "But I know now Ella didn't poison Esther."

Lizzie's expression shifted from concern to confusion. "What are you talking about?"

Jacob placed the crumpled note in front of her. "Ella thought she may have mixed up her order, but I've checked. This was Esther's last order. Not a single herb here could have harmed her. Ella didn't mix up the wrong ingredients. Someone else poisoned your grandmother if that is what caused her demise."

Lizzie's face paled as she stared at the note. The weight of the revelation settled between them like a thick fog. The thought of sweet Ella thinking she harmed her grandmother sickened Lizzie.

Evert, who had been standing off to the side, crossed his arms. "That still doesn't explain where she is."

Jacob swallowed hard. "Ura is on his way to Willow Springs."

The room fell into a stunned silence.

"Coming?" The word escaped her lips, quiet as a prayer.

Jacob nodded. "I just got a letter from my *bruder* in Wisconsin. He heard Ura had business in Pennsylvania and wasn't returning until he found Ella. I fear she's already in his grasp…"

Evert didn't wait for him to finish. He grabbed his coat, determination flashing in his eyes. "Then we'd better find her fast."

Lizzie's fingers trembled as she clutched the counter for support. "How did he know where to find her?"

Jacob let out a deep sigh. "I'm certain Amos had something to do with that."

***

As the front door of *Simply Yarn* clicked shut behind Jacob and Evert, the silence settled around Lizzie as she reached for her grandmother's journal. If someone had gone to such lengths to leave a warning, then there had to be more. She flipped through the pages, her eyes scanning each entry with new urgency. One passage she hadn't seen before made her heart stop.

October 4th

I promised Rebecca I'd protect her reputation, that I'd ensure Evert never knew what they had done, what had forced them to leave. I only wish she'd left before Amos got his claws in her. Before they were too deep in his schemes to ever break free.

Lizzie's pulse pounded in her ears.

Her grandmother had protected Evert from the truth his entire life... but why?

She walked back to the cottage and to the roll-topped desk to search its drawers one more time. There, tucked between old invoices, was an older, more delicate journal. The binding was faded, and the ink had bled in places. She carefully opened the fragile journal, her hands trembling as she found a letter from Rebecca.

Nathan thinks we can still get out, but it's too late. Amos knows. He will never let us leave without a price. I'm terrified. What have we done?

Lizzie swallowed hard.

What had they done?

She read on…

Nathan says we should run. But I told him if we do, we'll be hunted like dogs. We owe him too much. We should never have believed in Amos's promises.

He swore we'd be rich, that the business would thrive, that it was a simple investment. But we were fools. Amos's "Amish-made" goods were never ours to sell. He bought them from Englisch suppliers, passed them off as handmade, and made a fortune and pulled us in with him. Nathan believed his quick-rich schemes and now we're in too deep. Ach, Esther, I fear we will never be free from our past, and I'll never see my boy grow up. What have I done? We will never be free to live among our People again.

Lizzie clamped a hand over her mouth.

Her grandmother had known.

That's why Esther had spent her final years watching Amos so closely, because she had witnessed what he did to Evert's parents. But it wasn't until the last sentence of Rebecca's letter that she fully understood.

The only way to save Evert is to leave him behind. If we come back for him, Amos will reveal our part in his plans. Our parents will never understand. We have to disappear in order to save our families from more embarrassment.

Lizzie slammed the book shut, her mind reeling. Her grandmother had spent decades carrying this burden. She had tried to protect Evert from the truth, not just about his parents but about the real reason they left. Because they were afraid of Amos and fearful the Amish community would never accept them back into the fold.

Lizzie pressed the journal to her chest, tears stinging her eyes. Esther had been trying to warn Evert before she died. She had written to the bishop, preparing to expose Amos and the schemes he built his fortune on. And it may have cost her life.

Lizzie drew in a shaky breath. It was time to stop being afraid. Time to stop hesitating. She set the journal down and reached for the letter Esther had written to the bishop.

If her grandmother had been willing to risk everything for the truth, Lizzie wouldn't back down now. She was going to deliver the letter.

Tracy Fredrychowski

CHAPTER 14

The dim light from the small window seeped into the cramped stockroom, where Ella sat bound. The cold from the cement floor seeped through her dress, chilling her to the bone, but it was nothing compared to the icy fear twisting in her gut. She had spent the last few hours straining to hear the murmured conversations outside, catching only fragments... *Evert's name. Esther's. Something about time running out.*

Then the door creaked open.

Ura stepped inside, his boots scuffing against the floor as he approached. He looked calm, almost smug, as if he'd already won. He carried himself with the confidence of a man who believed he had full control. That alone set off warning bells in Ella's mind. She swallowed hard as he removed the rag covering her mouth, schooling her expression into one of reluctant surrender.

"Ura," she whispered, voice trembling just enough to seem

genuine. "How did you find me?"

He crouched in front of her, hands resting on his knees as he studied her. "You should know by now, there ain't no running from me." His voice was softer than she expected, even coaxing, but she knew better than to believe he had changed.

"I didn't mean to run. I just—" she let out a shaky breath. "I thought if I left, it would make things easier for both of us."

Ura let out a slow sigh and reached into his pocket, pulling out a small knife. Ella tensed, but instead of using it against her, he flicked it open and began sawing through the ropes binding her wrists. "You made things real hard for yourself, coming here. I've spent months tracking you down. If it weren't for Amos giving me a little nudge in the right direction, who knows how long it would've taken?"

So that was how he found her. Amos. The confirmation made her blood run cold, but she kept her features controlled.

Ura continued, voice slipping into something close to affection. "Your father promised you to me, and I intend to take back what is mine to have."

Ella swallowed down her revulsion, forcing herself to nod. "I just needed time to think," she said, rubbing her freed wrists. "But you're right. I can't stay here."

His gaze sharpened, like he was trying to decide if she was telling the truth. She shifted slightly, looking away as if ashamed, hoping it would sell the act.

"I just... I was afraid, Ura," she whispered. "But now I see there's no real choice, is there?" She peeked up at him through her lashes, trying to keep the hope in her chest from showing. "If I come back willingly, will you give me time? You know... to get used to things?"

Ura's lips curled into something resembling a smile. "Of course. I'm no monster."

Oh, but you are, she thought, biting back the retort. She had to play this carefully.

"*Goot*," she murmured. "Then I'll come willingly."

Ura leaned in, brushing a strand of hair from her cheek. Ella fought the urge to flinch.

"That's my girl," he murmured.

She forced a smile. But inside, she was screaming.

***

The night air was crisp as Ura walked beside Ella, his hand hovering too close to her back for comfort. The responsibility of her deception settled heavily on her chest, but she forced herself to keep pace, matching his steps as they made their way toward the heart of Willow Springs.

"I'll just grab a few things from my room first," Ura said casually, nodding toward the small inn at the edge of town.

Ella hesitated, the thought of stepping inside his space making her stomach churn. They shouldn't be alone together, not like this, not unless they were properly married. But she couldn't object without raising suspicion. She swallowed her discomfort and nodded stiffly. "Alright," she murmured.

The door creaked open, and she stepped inside after him, her gaze sweeping the modest hotel room. It was simple, no different than any other guest room she had ever seen. The air smelled faintly of charred metal and oil, an unmistakable scent that clung to Ura's clothes like a shadow of his past.

She knew that smell. It belonged to the forge. Ella kept her face neutral, her hands clasped tightly in front of her to keep them from trembling as Ura gathered a few items from his duffle bag.

He slung the bag over his shoulder and took a step toward her. "I need to tidy up some business, and you're coming with me."

She nodded, hoping he wouldn't sense her anxiety.

He studied her for a long moment before letting out a slow breath. "Fine," he said at last, but something was unsettling in his tone... something that made the fine hairs on the back of her neck prickle. "I'm not letting you out of my sight, so don't get any ideas; I won't tolerate you running off again."

"I understand," she whispered, lowering her gaze.

He lifted a hand to her chin, tilting her face back up until their eyes met. "*Goot*," he said tenderly, though the steel beneath his voice was unmistakable.

She forced herself to stay calm, to keep her breathing even.

Ura studied her for another beat, then at last turned toward the small wooden dresser beside the bed. Ella's eyes flickered over the room once more as he reached for something inside the top drawer.

That's when she saw it. Half-tucked beneath a folded handkerchief. Her stomach twisted. Why would he bring something like that all the way from Wisconsin?

She just had a second to process before Ura turned back, stuffing something small into his pocket before slamming the drawer shut. The sound made her flinch, but she quickly masked it with a nod as he gestured for her to move toward the door.

"Come on, then," he said, his voice deceptively calm.

***

The sky had deepened to an inky black, speckled with stars, by the time Lizzie hooked up her buggy horse for the two-mile drive to Bishop Schrock's farm. The crisp night air nipped at her cheeks, and the quiet clip-clop of her horse's hooves against the blacktop was the only sound breaking the silence.

This couldn't wait, not until morning. Amos had deceived their community for too long, and her *grossmommi* had given her the proof to stop him. Lizzie clutched the letter tightly in her lap, whispering a prayer as she guided the buggy forward. *"Lord, let this be enough. Let it stop him before he can do anything else to hurt us."*

Her thoughts drifted to Evert and Jacob, out searching for Ella in the dead of night. Worry gnawed at her stomach. Where was she? And why had she disappeared so suddenly?

As Lizzie neared the bishop's farm, the soft glow of oil lamps from the house highlighted the neatly kept yard. The white farmhouse sat just across the road from the *Apple*

Blossom Inn, a place that always seemed warm and inviting, even at this late hour.

She pulled the buggy to a stop and hopped down, tying her horse to the hitching post. Gravel crunched under her shoes as she approached the front steps. Before she could knock, the heavy wooden door creaked open.

Maggie Schrock, the bishop's *fraa*, smiled warmly at her. "*Ach*, Lizzie. What a surprise at this hour. Come in, child, it's too cold to be standing out there."

Lizzie stepped inside, the heat from the woodstove instantly soothing her chilled skin. The smell of fresh bread lingered in the air, and a quilt lay draped over a rocking chair near the fire; a scene so peaceful it made Lizzie yearn for all this to be over.

"Is the bishop still awake?" she asked, glancing toward the study.

Maggie nodded, concern flashing in her kind eyes. "*Jah*, he's just finishing his evening reading. Go on in; he'll be glad to see you."

Lizzie took a steady breath and walked toward the open doorway. Inside, Bishop Schrock sat at his desk, flipping through the worn pages of his Bible. He looked up at her entrance, setting the book aside.

"Lizzie," he greeted, his deep voice steady. "What brings you here so late?"

She hesitated for only a moment before stepping forward, extending the letter toward him. "It's from my *grossmommi*. She wrote it before she died. I think it's important you see it."

The bishop took the letter, his brow furrowing as he unfolded the paper. Silence stretched between them as his eyes moved over the handwritten words, his expression darkening with each line.

Lizzie clasped her hands together. "I know Amos has been dishonest in his business, but this... this letter confirms it. *Grossmommi* feared what would happen if he wasn't stopped."

Bishop Schrock let out a heavy sigh and folded the letter thoroughly. "Lizzie, this is not the first time concerns about Amos have come to my attention. Others have voiced suspicions, but none have come forward with proof like this."

"Then we have to do something," she urged, her voice firm. "Amos is dangerous, and I fear he's behind more than just dishonest business."

The bishop rubbed his temple, then gave her a grave nod. "It's time we take action. I'll speak with the ministers first thing in the morning, but most likely, Amos will be placed under the

Bann until he repents and makes right what he's done. If he refuses... then he will be shunned."

Relief flooded through Lizzie, but it was short-lived. Amos wouldn't take this quietly. And that thought sent a shiver of unease straight through her.

***

Ella forced herself to move with steady, measured steps as she entered the small upstairs apartment above the shop. The familiar scent of dried rose leaves and chamomile filled the space, a stark contrast to the suffocating tension pressing down on her. Her uncle wasn't home. That was a relief.

Ura dropped his bag by the door, rubbing the back of his neck as he exhaled harshly. "Hurry up. Grab your things. You won't be coming back here again." His voice was clipped, his tone final.

Ella's fingers curled at her sides, but she forced herself to remain calm. She had expected this. He wanted control, just as he always had.

She turned to her small chest of drawers, carefully pulling open the top one. Her belongings were few, just the dresses she had brought with her from Wisconsin, a couple of simple shawls, and a bonnet that had seen better days. She reached for her travel bag and hesitated before slowly gathering her things.

Behind her, Ura slumped against the doorway, watching her with sharp, assessing eyes. "And don't pack anything you bought here. Take only what you came with."

Ella stiffened, but she didn't argue. That wasn't the battle to fight right now.

Instead, she turned to him, lifting her chin slightly. "And where exactly do you expect me to stay?"

Ura smirked, his arms folding over his broad chest. "With me, of course."

Ella swallowed against the bile rising in her throat. "We're not married, it wouldn't be proper."

His smirk deepened, twisting into something darker. "*Ach,* don't flatter yourself, I have no intention of taking advantage of you before you're fully mine." His voice dripped with condescension, but she didn't miss the edge in it... the possessive undertone that made her skin crawl.

A shiver ran down her spine as she averted her gaze, focusing on folding her dresses neatly instead of reacting to his words. She had learned the hard way not to question him.

222

Her mind flashed to the letters she had found months ago, the ones tucked away in his locked drawer back in Wisconsin. Letters from an *Englisher* woman, pleading with him, warning him. The words had made her blush even as they had left a deep, unsettled feeling in her gut.

Ura had a secretive side. A dangerous side. And she wasn't about to find herself trapped in it again. She took a steady breath and forced herself to move, keeping her expression blank as she folded the last of her things into her satchel. She hesitated at the herb book in her drawer, thumbing through its pages before setting it aside.

She would go with him. But only long enough to figure out his true motives, and how to escape them.

***

Lizzie sat at the worn wooden table, her fingers wrapped around a cup of tea that had long gone cold. The impact of the evening pressed down on her, but she forced herself to keep her thoughts steady.

The back door creaked open, and Evert stepped inside, his expression a mix of frustration and exhaustion. He shut the door behind him, his shoulders sagging as he removed his hat and ran a hand through his dark hair.

Lizzie didn't need to ask. She could see it in his eyes. "Nothing?" she said softly.

Evert let out a heavy sigh and reclined against the counter, shaking his head. "We searched everywhere. Checked the back roads, the barns, even Amos's warehouse." He scrubbed a hand over his jaw. "Jacob and I were sure we'd find something... anything to prove Amos was behind this. But either he's better at covering his tracks than I thought, or we're looking in the wrong places."

Lizzie set her cup down, folding her hands in her lap. "Did he seem nervous?"

Evert gave a dry, humorless chuckle. "Oh, he was plenty nervous. Even tried to play it cool, but I could see it, and he knows more than he's letting on. But without proof, we've got nothing to hold over him."

Lizzie straightened. "I took *Grossmommi's* letter to Bishop Schrock."

Evert's head snapped up. "You did?"

She nodded. "I drove over after closing the shop. He read the letter and agreed it's time Amos was dealt with. The ministers will be paying him a visit in the morning. And…" she hesitated, her next words thick with meaning, "Bishop Schrock asked us both to meet him at nine. He wants us to explain everything we've found so far… with Amos present."

Evert pushed away from the counter, crossing his arms. "So, we finally have a chance to make him answer for what he's done." He shook his head, a bitter edge in his voice. "I just wish we had more. More than a letter. More than suspicions. Something concrete to prove what he did to Esther."

Lizzie exhaled, her chest tight. "At least justice will be served, at least as it goes in an Amish community."

Evert sighed, nodding. "That's something."

A quiet moment passed, and Lizzie studied him as he stared at the knots in the wood floor, lost in thought. She had never seen him so conflicted.

"What's next for you?" she whispered.

Evert looked up, meeting her gaze with something unreadable in his expression. "Now that you know who your parents are, and we're about to get Amos out of the picture… where will you go?"

Evert held her gaze for a long moment before shifting, rubbing the back of his neck. "I guess that depends."

"On what?"

His lips quirked, but there was no teasing in his voice. "On whether I have a reason to stay."

Lizzie's fingers tightened around her cup. She hadn't expected him to say it outright, to hint at something more than just his search for truth.

She swallowed, looking down at the flickering lamp's glow. "Evert... I have no desire to leave my Amish heritage." She lifted her eyes, steady and unwavering. "It would take time, you know. A lot of time. For you. For the bishop. To decide if you even have what it takes to return if that's what you are hoping for."

Evert studied her, his expression unreadable. Then he nodded, a slow, contemplative nod. "I know."

Silence stretched between them, but it wasn't empty. It was filled with possibilities, with choices yet to be made, with unspoken words hovering in the air.

Finally, he pushed off the counter, his voice softer now. "I should go. Get some sleep before tomorrow."

Lizzie stood as well, walking him to the door. "Good night, Evert."

As the door shut behind him, she pressed her hand against

the wood, closing her eyes. She didn't know what the future held. But for the first time, she wasn't afraid to find out.

***

Ella's hands trembled as she eased open the top drawer of the wooden dresser, glancing quickly toward the closed bathroom door. The faint sound of running water masked the rustling of papers beneath her fingertips. She knew she had only minutes, maybe even less.

Her heart pounded in her chest as she pushed aside a stack of folded handkerchiefs. Her fingers skimmed the edges of what felt like a small container. Swallowing hard, she lifted it out.

Her stomach twisted. She had seen this before, back home in Wisconsin. A blacksmith's solvent. She had watched Ura use it countless times, the distinct, acrid smell clinging to his clothes when he worked.

A folded slip of paper beneath the container caught her eye. Her fingers moved fast, unfolding it with measured desperation. Ella's breath stilled in her throat.

A cold dread slithered down her spine. Suddenly a shadow loomed over her. Before she could turn, Ura's fingers closed around her wrist, yanking her backward with a force that sent the paper fluttering from her hand.

She gasped, her pulse hammering as she spun to face him. His stormy eyes bore into hers, dark and unreadable. His grip was tight, almost bruising, and for the first time since her arrival in Willow Springs, true fear knotted in her chest.

"What," Ura said in a low, dangerous voice, "do you think you're doing?"

Ella struggled to find words, to think of a lie, but she knew she had been caught.

And by the look in Ura's eyes, he knew it too.

CHAPTER 15

Jacob stood in the doorway of Lizzie's shop, his hat clenched tightly in his hands. The burden of worry had deepened the lines on his face, and his usually steady voice was strained.

"She never came home," his gaze darting between Lizzie and Evert, who had just stepped into the shop behind him.

Lizzie's stomach twisted. "Oh… Jacob."

Jacob gave a firm nod and stepped inside, unfolding a familiar leather-bound book from under his arm: the *Stutzman Family Herbal Remedies*.

"She left this behind," he said grimly. "I gave her this book. She'd never leave it behind unless—" He stopped himself, his gut tightening.

Lizzie finished his sentence. "—unless she was in trouble."

Jacob flipped open the book, revealing two deliberately folded page corners: a clear and intentional sign, something Ella would never have done unless she was trying to send a message.

She treasured the book and would never fold a page over. He pointed to the first dog-eared page. "This page is for an herbal antidote used for treating poisoning."

Lizzie sucked in a sharp breath. "You think she's trying to tell us she's been poisoned?"

Jacob shook his head. "Not necessarily, but she's warning us about something. This could be her way of telling me she's not safe. That she needs help."

Evert leaned in, studying the second folded page. His jaw clenched as he read the heading. "Wild Indigo Root."

Jacob frowned. "That doesn't make any sense. It's not something we keep stocked regularly, and it has nothing to do with poisoning."

Lizzie flipped back and forth between the pages, trying to make sense of it. Her pulse quickened when her eyes fell on the bottom of the first page. "Look at the page number."

Evert and Jacob both leaned in.

"Two-oh-eight," Evert read aloud, his brows pulling together.

Lizzie met his gaze, she mouthed the words more than spoke them. "Route 208."

The realization hit them all at once.

"She's telling us where she is," Lizzie said, gripping the book. "*Root's Motel* on Route 208. She's trying to get a message to us, I'm sure of it!"

Evert glanced at the old wooden clock above the counter.

"We have just enough time," he muttered, shoving a hand through his hair.

Jacob shot him a confused look. "Time for what?"

Evert turned to Jacob, his voice firm. "The meeting with Bishop Schrock and the ministers. Lizzie took her grandmother's letter to the bishop last night. He wants us there when they confront Amos."

Jacob's lips parted a little as if torn between urgency for Ella and the impact of what was about to happen. "Now?"

Evert nodded. "We need to see this through. Amos is at the center of this mess. We take him down today, and then we focus everything on finding Ella."

Jacob hesitated, gripping the herbal book tightly in his hands. "I don't like the thought of waiting, knowing she could be in danger."

Lizzie turned toward Jacob. "This won't take long."

Jacob exhaled slowly, his fingers tightening around the book. At last, he gave a curt nod.

***

Evert drummed his fingers against the steering wheel; his gaze locked on *Zook Wholesale Supply's* dark windows across the street. Its large wooden sign hanging askew above the entrance.

Beside him, Lizzie shifted in her seat, pulling her shawl tighter around her shoulders. "Do you think he has any idea what's coming?"

Evert scoffed. "Amos always thinks he's one step ahead." He glanced at Jacob, who sat tense, gripping the herbal book Ella had left behind like a lifeline. "But today, he's wrong."

Jacob's expression remained grim. "I don't care about Amos. I care about finding Ella."

A buggy pulled up near the entrance of Amos's office. Bishop Schrock stepped down, his usual calm demeanor shadowed by the weight of the task at hand. Two ministers followed, their expressions somber as they adjusted their hats against the brisk wind.

"That's our cue." Evert turned the truck off and stepped out. Lizzie and Jacob followed, crossing the street with purpose as they trailed behind the ministers into Zook's office.

***

Amos sat behind a large oak desk, shuffling invoices and barely glancing up as the door swung open.

"This had better be good," he muttered, tossing a stack of papers aside. "I don't have time for..." His gaze lifted, his sneer faltering when he saw Bishop Schrock flanked by the ministers, and then Evert, Lizzie, and Jacob standing just behind them.

Amos leaned back in his chair, a smirk tugging at the corner of his mouth. "*Ach*, I figured this day would come. You finally decided to stick your noses where they don't belong?"

Bishop Schrock ignored the provocation. "We have solid proof that you have been running an illegal merchandising business for years; passing off counterfeit goods as Amish-made, deceiving both the community and the *Englisch* buyers who trust us."

Amos's smirk didn't waver. "What proof?"

The Bishop stepped forward and placed the letter from Esther on the desk. "This."

For the first time, Amos hesitated. His beady eyes darted to the paper, his fingers curling into fists on the desk's surface.

Bishop Schrock pressed on. "We've known for too long that your dealings weren't right, but we turned a blind eye, hoping you'd correct your course. But with this... " He tapped the letter. "... we can no longer stand by. You are being placed under the *Bann*. Effective immediately."

The smirk vanished. Amos slammed his palm onto the desk, his chair scraping backward as he stood. "You can't do that."

"It is already done."

"You think you can just cut me off?" Amos's face twisted with fury. "I built this business. I brought in money for the community. I created jobs! And now, because of a dead woman's letter and a few stubborn kids meddling in what they don't understand, you think you can take it all away?"

His gaze snapped to Evert, dark and filled with rage. "This is your fault."

Evert held his ground. "Funny. I was thinking this was yours."

Amos scoffed, shaking his head. "You should've stayed away, Miller. None of this would have happened if you hadn't come sniffing around. Thomas and Miriam were handled long ago. And your precious Esther... " He sneered. "Should've been taken care of years ago."

A chill settled over the room. Lizzie sucked in a breath.

"You admit to harming her?" Jacob's voice was dangerously low.

Amos's smirk deepened. "I didn't have to. Someone else beat me to it."

The bishop squared his shoulders. "This is your last chance to repent and correct your way. If you don't, you'll lose everything."

Amos grabbed a stack of invoices and shoved them into a leather satchel. "I don't plan on sticking around for this nonsense."

Bishop Schrock shook his head. "This isn't just a warning. The community will no longer recognize you as one of us. Your business here is finished."

Amos let out a bitter laugh. "Then I'll move it somewhere else." His lips curled into a smug grin. "And don't you worry. I have plenty of friends in other places who won't care what I sell or how I got it."

Jacob stepped forward, his jaw clenched. "Where's Ella?"

Amos arched a brow, clearly amused. "*Ach*, why are you asking me? I don't keep track of every whiny girl who crosses my path." He smirked. "Besides, some people have more right to her than you do."

Jacob's face darkened. "What does that mean?"

Amos shrugged, his lips twisting into something unreadable. "Just that you shouldn't go looking too hard. Maybe she's exactly where she belongs."

Evert stepped in now, his voice dangerously low. "What do you know?"

Amos chuckled, a slow, knowing sound that sent a chill through the room. "Maybe you should be asking the right questions. You should have known she's not yours to keep."

Lizzie's stomach twisted. "What's that supposed to mean?"

Amos lifted his hands. "Don't look at me. I don't have the girl, and Jacob knows exactly what I'm talking about."

He yanked the office door open, slamming it behind him, but not before he added. "And you're looking in all the wrong places about Esther. I didn't touch her, but I wish I had put a stop to her meddling long ago."

The heavy silence left in Amos's wake pressed against the small office. The bishop exhaled, rubbing a hand over his beard as he turned toward Lizzie and Evert, his sharp gaze full of unspoken questions.

"What did Amos mean by that?" Bishop Schrock's voice was firm, yet there was something else in it... concern. "Are you telling me that you believe Esther's death was intentional? Not of natural causes?"

Lizzie and Evert exchanged a glance before Evert stepped forward. "We've had suspicions for some time now, but we haven't had any proof."

The bishop's brow furrowed deeply, his hands clasped behind his back as he paced. "This is not a light accusation. If harm was done, we must seek justice. The *Ordnung* teaches us to handle matters within the community, but I don't hold to the same rigid ways as the Old Order. If this was deliberate, I will not hesitate to involve the authorities." He stopped, his piercing gaze locking onto them. "Do you think we need to bring in Detective Powers?"

Lizzie hesitated, shifting uneasily. "We were hoping to have more to give him first. Right now, all we have are suspicions and scattered clues."

Bishop Schrock exhaled sharply. "Suspicion was enough to remove Amos from the community. But a life is an entirely different matter if that is what truly happened."

Jacob cleared his throat, stepping forward. "Right now, we

have a bigger problem to deal with."

The bishop turned his attention to him.

Jacob's face was grim, his fingers curling at his sides. "Ella is missing. She never came home last night," Jacob admitted, his voice strained. "She took all her things, but I know my niece. She left something behind, something that I believe was a message to tell me she was in trouble. I fear she has been taken against her will."

Bishop Schrock's lips pressed into a thin line. "Taken? By whom?"

Jacob swallowed hard. "I believe it may be Ura Hostetler from Cashton, Wisconsin. She was pledged to marry him, but didn't feel it was a good match and came here to escape such a union."

Evert stepped in. "Amos hinted that someone else had more of a right to Ella than Jacob. We think he was talking about Ura."

Lizzie's stomach twisted with worry, but she lifted her chin. "We have to find her, Bishop."

He nodded, his voice steady and firm. "Go. I'll go and get the authorities involved."

Jacob tucked the book into his pocket, and they turned and

hurried out of Amos's office, the toll of urgency pressing down on them.

***

The morning light crept through the heavy drapes of the musty motel room. Ella swallowed hard, forcing herself to stay calm as she watched Ura pace the floor, his frustration mounting with every call he made.

"I paid extra, what do you mean, you're delayed?"

Ella couldn't hear the response, but whatever was said didn't satisfy him. His nostrils flared, and he ran a hand through his dark, unruly hair before barking, "Fine." With an aggravated sigh, Ura slammed the phone onto the nightstand and turned to face her. His eyes were cold, calculating.

"We're leaving as soon as our ride gets here," his voice edged with finality.

Ella pressed her lips together, feigning compliance while her mind worked furiously. She needed to stall. Needed to get more information.

"You could've left me be. I'm sure there are other girls better suited to you. Why chase after me?" she asked, keeping her tone measured.

Ura let out a bitter chuckle, shaking his head as he leaned against the dresser, arms crossed over his chest. "You don't get it, do you? In the eyes of the community, you'll make the perfect cover. Sweet and innocent Ella Stutzman." He picked up a toothpick and balanced it between his teeth. "Luck was on my side as it just so happened you ran right in the middle of my next deal with Amos Zook."

She almost didn't press, but the words came out before she could stop them. "Why Amos Zook?"

"He needed someone to move his shipments quietly. Someone who could slip things in and out of Amish settlements without raising suspicion, and he heard of me from another community."

Ella's mind reeled. "You were helping him smuggle fake goods?"

Ura's gaze darkened. "I didn't think of it that way. I was just a middleman. But then Esther Yoder stuck her nose where it didn't belong."

Ura exhaled angrily, rubbing his temples as if recalling the memory pained him. "She wrote me a letter, warning me to stay out of Willow Springs or she'd expose everything to my father."

Ella's stomach twisted as she remembered the folded letter she had found among Ura's things. She had hardly had time to skim it before he caught her snooping, but the words *"You've done enough damage, stay away from Ella or I'll make sure everyone knows"* had been burned into her mind.

She forced herself to stay calm as she asked the question she already knew the answer to.

"Did you... did you have anything to do with Esther's death?"

Ura's expression shifted; something sinister flickered in his eyes. He stepped closer, his presence suffocating. "You ask too many questions."

She swallowed, willing herself not to recoil. "Answer me."

Ura smirked. "Let's just say... I did what needed to be done."

Ella gasped quietly. The cleaning solvent. The one she had found in his belongings. It had been out of place, suspicious. Now, it made sense.

"I couldn't let her ruin everything," Ura continued, his voice dangerously low. "She thought she could scare me away, but she underestimated just how far I'd go to protect what's mine."

Ella's heart pounded in her chest. He had poisoned Esther.

"You—you killed her," she whispered, barely able to form the words.

Ella's blood turned to ice. "You won't get away with this," she said, her voice shaking despite her fear of him.

Ura grabbed her chin roughly, forcing her to look into his cold, unfeeling eyes. "Once we're married, you won't have a choice but to keep quiet."

Ella clenched her fists, her nails digging into her palms. She had to escape and warn Lizzie and Evert before they got too close to the truth.

CHAPTER 16

Evert's hands tightened around the steering wheel as he eased the truck to a stop across the street from the rundown motel. The neon "VACANCY" sign buzzed, flickering intermittently in the dim morning light. A steady drizzle dampened the pavement, mixing with the scent of wet asphalt and livestock from the nearby *Feed & Seed*.

Jacob sat in the passenger seat, his fingers drumming anxiously against his knee. "If she's here, we'll know soon enough. Not many Amish drivers around here, and I'd recognize most of their cars if they drove in."

Lizzie sat in the back, her stomach twisted in knots. "What if we're wrong?" she whispered. "What if he's already taken her somewhere else?"

Jacob shook his head. "No. Amos knew more than he let on. And who else could he have meant when he said 'some people have more right to her than I do?'" His voice darkened. "It has to be Ura."

Evert exhaled sharply, keeping his eyes trained on the motel. "We don't move until we know for sure."

A tense silence stretched between them. Jacob rubbed his hands together, his fingers twitching. "She's just a girl. I—" he hesitated, his voice thick with emotion. "I never had children of my own. But I've looked after Ella as if she were mine these last six months. If he's hurt her… " He clenched his jaw, unable to finish.

A vehicle rumbled into the parking lot, its headlights slicing through the mist. A dark passenger van. The kind used for long-distance travel. It rolled to a stop in front of the farthest motel room.

The door to the room swung open. An Amish dressed man stepped outside, adjusting his coat against the chill, his eyes scanning the lot before landing on the van. He muttered something to the driver, his movements rushed, anxious.

Then Lizzie saw Ella. She stood in the doorway, her hands clasped in front of her. Her face was pale, her eyes darting from the van to Ura, then hesitating, just briefly before locking with Lizzie's. A silent plea.

Lizzie's breath caught. *She's terrified.*

"Hold on," Evert murmured, putting the truck in gear. He maneuvered the vehicle across the lot, rolling to a stop directly behind the passenger van, blocking its exit.

Ura stiffened at the sight of them, his body going rigid. His lips curled in a sneer as he took a few slow steps forward, the rain misting his face.

"This is none of your concern," he called, his voice dangerously calm. "I'm taking back what's rightfully mine."

Jacob threw open the truck door, his boots splashing against the wet pavement as he stepped out. "Ella's not a piece of property."

"She's been bequeathed to me," Ura shot back, his hand twitching at his side. "She belongs to me."

Evert stepped out next, his stance rigid. "That's not how this works," he said, his voice steady.

Lizzie scarcely breathed, her focus trained on Ella, who still hadn't moved.

Ura turned toward the driver. "Get my bag."

Evert moved swiftly, stepping between the driver and the vehicle door. "Not happening."

The driver hesitated, realizing there was nowhere to go.

Ura turned back toward Ella, his voice lowering into a

growl. "Get in the van. Now!"

Ella flinched.

"No," Lizzie said, stepping forward before she could stop herself. "You don't have the right to force her."

Ura's eyes snapped to her, narrowing. "You should stay out of things you don't understand."

Jacob's voice wavered with restrained anger. "You're not taking her."

Ura's gaze flicked back toward Ella, his face hardening.

And then, in a moment of pure defiance, Ella found her voice. "He poisoned Esther."

The words hung in the air like a curse.

Lizzie's stomach twisted, the breath knocked from her chest.

Evert's body went rigid. "What did you just say?" His voice was dangerously calm.

Ura's face contorted in fury. He lunged toward Ella, grabbing her wrist.

"You need to keep your mouth shut," he growled.

Jacob surged forward. "Let her go!"

Evert was faster.

With a surge of motion, he reached for Ura, grabbing the

collar of his coat and yanking him backward. Ura stumbled, releasing Ella in the process.

Ella scrambled away, falling into Lizzie's waiting arms.

The sirens grew louder. Closer.

Ura turned, his eyes wild. "This isn't over."

Evert didn't budge. "Yes. It is."

Red and blue lights flashed across the motel lot as two police cruisers skidded to a stop.

Detective Powers was the first out. "Hands where I can see them!"

Ura's face twisted in frustration, his hands slowly lifting into the air.

Ella buried her face into Lizzie's shoulder, trembling.

"It's over," Lizzie whispered, holding her tight. "You're safe now."

Tracy Fredrychowski

CHAPTER 17

The moving truck rumbled down the street, disappearing into the gray morning light, carrying away the last remnants of the life they had built in Erie. Miriam stood in the doorway of their now-empty shop, arms crossed over her chest. For nearly two decades, this shop had been her world. A safe place. A new beginning. But it had never truly been home.

Beside her, Thomas exhaled sharply, his posture rigid as he stared at the empty sidewalk. "Feels like we're running again." Miriam turned to him, her heart aching at the hard lines of his face. "Maybe it feels that way, but this time, we're running *toward* something instead of away."

Thomas sighed. "I can't believe you've talked me into retuning there." His blue eyes, so much like Evert's, burned with an anger that had long since settled into resentment. "You want to go back like everything is fine? Like they didn't cast us out? Like we weren't shunned and treated like traitors for choosing a different life? I spent years trying to forget the way they looked at us when we left. Like we were *nothing*."

Miriam sighed, reaching for his arm, but he pulled away. "Thomas, that was thirty years ago."

"And you think thirty years changes anything?" he spat. "You think those people will welcome us back with open arms? No. They'll whisper behind our backs. They'll remind us that we never should've left."

She shook her head. "The People we knew then... most of them are gone, Thomas. Our parents. The elders who disapproved of us. They aren't there anymore. The ghosts of our past aren't waiting for us in Willow Springs."

His clenched jaw told her he wasn't convinced.

"Besides, we're not going back to Willow Springs but to New Castle. It's on the outskirts, far enough away that no one will remember us, but close enough that we could be involved in Evert's life—*if* he lets us."

Thomas let out a low, frustrated breath and rubbed a hand over his face. She could see the battle waging inside him. The part of him that still carried the wounds of rejection and the part of him that longed for something more, even if he wasn't ready to admit it.

Miriam pressed on in a hushed tone. "I know we can't go back to being Amish. We've been English for too long. But that doesn't mean we can't go *home*."

His eyes flicked to hers, something unreadable shifting in his gaze. She saw hesitation. Longing. But most of all, fear.

"*Home*," he repeated, the word heavy on his tongue.

She nodded. "Yes. For you. For me. And for Evert."

Thomas let out a bitter chuckle. "You think he wants anything to do with us? The boy we abandoned?"

Miriam swallowed hard. "I don't know. But I know that if we don't try, we'll regret it for the rest of our lives."

A long silence stretched between them. The hum of the city moved around them, but Miriam heard nothing but the sound of Thomas's quiet, heavy breaths.

Finally, he exhaled and gave a slow, reluctant nod. "If I do this, it's not for me," he muttered. "And not for Willow Springs. It's for you. And maybe... *maybe* for him."

Miriam's heart swelled with hope. She reached for his hand, and this time, he didn't pull away. "Then let's go home."

She could see his mind working, and after a moment, she dared to add, "And you know... you've always talked about that little farm you wanted. A place to plant some vegetables, raise a few animals, maybe a draft horse just like the ones your father had."

Thomas's brow furrowed, and for the first time in a long time, he looked thoughtful instead of bitter.

"You're not getting any younger, Thomas," she teased softly. "Why not use these years to enjoy the kind of life you always dreamed about? A simple life. One you never got to have when you were a boy, working yourself into the ground just to prove you were enough for your father."

He let out a breath, and something in his shoulders relaxed. The idea wasn't completely unwelcome.

Miriam nudged him gently. "And I'd love to do something meaningful too. If Lizzie would have me, I'd love to help at *Simply Yarn*. Maybe teach the younger women how to crochet or knit. Pass down some of the things Esther taught me."

The mention of Esther's name softened the hard edges of Thomas's face.

She squeezed his hand. "I know we made mistakes. But there's still time to do something good with the life we have left."

Thomas was silent for a long moment before nodding slowly. "New Castle," he murmured. "Far enough away… but close enough to try."

Miriam smiled, tears welling in her eyes. "*Jah*. Close enough to try."

And with that, the door to their future creaked open just enough to let the light in.

***

Detective Powers sat at Lizzie's worn wooden kitchen table, his hands clasped together as he looked between Evert, Lizzie, Jacob, and Ella. The steam from Lizzie's freshly brewed coffee curled in the air, but no one reached for their mugs, their attention solely fixed on the detective.

"Well," Powers exhaled, rubbing the back of his neck. "It looks like you all got tangled up in something bigger than you ever realized." He glanced at Evert. "We've been trying to nail Amos Zook for fraud and forgery for some time. We knew he was running an illegal business, smuggling non-Amish goods and selling them under the guise of handcrafted merchandise. What we didn't know was how deep it ran."

Evert leaned forward, his jaw tight. "And Ura?"

Powers smirked grimly. "Oh, he sang like a canary the

second we put the pressure on him. He was desperate to cut a deal, but with everything we have on him: kidnapping, attempted trafficking, and let's not forget... *murder.* He's not walking free for sure." The detective shook his head. "Ura won't see the light of day for a long, long time, if ever."

Jacob let out a slow breath, glancing at Ella with relief in his eyes.

"And Amos?" Lizzie asked.

"He's got a mess of charges stacked against him: fraud, smuggling, extortion. The Feds are interested now. He's going to be answering to more than just me." Powers chuckled dryly. "One thing is for sure: He won't be coming back to Willow Springs anytime soon, thanks to the cooperation of Jacob Miller, and Thomas and Miriam Mast."

A weight seemed to lift off the room. Lizzie closed her eyes briefly, whispering a silent prayer of gratitude. The nightmare was definitely over.

Detective Powers stood, reaching for his hat. "I just wanted to give you all an update before the news spreads. It's over. You can all breathe easy now."

As he turned to leave, he stopped and pointed a finger at Lizzie and Evert. "And next time, leave the sleuthing to the professionals."

Lizzie grinned. "No promises."

With a shake of his head and a muttered chuckle, the detective left, closing the door behind him.

A few moments of silence stretched between them before Lizzie turned to Ella. "What about you? What are you going to do now?"

Ella hesitated, looking at Jacob. "I miss my family." Her voice was soft but sure. "And now that it's safe, I want to go home to Wisconsin."

Jacob's lips pressed together, and for a moment, Lizzie saw something like sadness in his eyes. But then he nodded, his expression shifting to something more prideful. "You've got skills, Ella. You always have. You should use them."

"I will," Ella said. "I want to open my own herb shop. Bring natural healing to my community."

Jacob cleared his throat and nodded. "*Goot.* You'll make your *datt* proud."

Lizzie felt her heart swell as she watched Jacob and Ella share a moment of understanding.

After Ella and Jacob said their goodbyes and left, Lizzie turned to Evert. "Now that Esther's death has been solved, where do you go from here?"

Evert's lips curled into a small smirk. "Funny you should ask."

Lizzie arched a brow, waiting.

"My uncle left me a plot of land near Mast Lumber." He watched her carefully. "I plan to build a house out there, next to Isaiah's place up on the hill."

Lizzie's heart skipped, but she masked her reaction. "Oh? That's a big step."

He nodded. "*Jah*. And I'll need some help."

Lizzie furrowed her brows. "Help?"

Evert pushed away from the counter and stepped closer. "A house should be designed to suit its future occupants, wouldn't you agree?"

Lizzie's cheeks warmed. "I suppose."

He grinned. "So, I was wondering… who better to ask than someone who might have an opinion on it?"

Lizzie folded her arms. "And why would *I* have an opinion?"

Evert's smirk deepened. "Because once I get settled… once I meet with Bishop Schrock and start working my way back into the community…" He hesitated, then let his voice drop softer.

"I'd like to court you properly. That is, without my truck and in proper Amish attire."

Lizzie's breath caught, but she held her ground. "That's a big commitment."

He nodded. "*Jah*, it is." His expression grew serious. "But it's one I'm willing to make... *if* you'll give me the chance."

Lizzie searched his eyes, her heart fluttering in a way that felt both exciting and terrifying. Finally, she smiled. "We'll see."

Evert chuckled, stepping back. "Fair enough."

Before he could grab his hat, he paused for a moment before turning to her again. "And what about you? Do you plan to keep the shop if you ever marry?"

Lizzie hesitated, the answer settling deep within her. "All I've ever wanted is family. Maybe someday, I'll find someone to take over the shop, freeing me to have the big family I've always dreamed of."

Evert studied her, a slow smile forming. "Then I guess we both have something to work toward."

Lizzie watched him, her heart full, knowing that for the first time in a long time, everything was falling into place.

And maybe, just maybe, her future had Evert Miller in it

after all.

***

Jacob stood with his hands deep in his pockets, his face a mixture of pride and worry as he watched Ella prepare to board the bus back to Wisconsin. The early morning air carried a hint of winter, crisp and full of promise.

"You know," he said, his voice thick with emotion, "you've been like a daughter to me. I hate to see you go, but I know your heart has been longing for home."

Ella swallowed hard, adjusting the strap of her bag over her shoulder. "I never thought I'd be ready to go back, but I am now. Because you believed in me."

Jacob smiled, though his eyes betrayed the sadness he felt. "Take life one day at a time," he told her. "Your story isn't finished yet." He reached into his coat pocket and handed her a delicately wrapped bundle. "Inside this are my favorite herbal blends; the ones I've taught you how to mix. Start small, one tincture at a time, and build your dream the way you always wanted."

Ella's eyes welled with tears. She hugged the bundle to her

chest, nodding. "I will."

Jacob took a deep breath. "Now, go on. You've got a bus to catch."

She stepped onto the bus and found a seat by the window. As she settled in, she turned to wave at Jacob, but just as she did, a young Amish man sat down beside her.

"Cashton, huh?" he said, offering her a friendly smile. His voice was warm, steady, and filled with an easy confidence.

Ella nodded, taking in his strong, work-worn hands and the slight ruffle in his shirt from an early morning start. He had the look of someone who worked the land.

"*Jah*," she replied. "It's home."

"I hear it's nice," he said, adjusting the satchel in his lap. "Just bought a farm outside of Cashton. The soil's good, or so I'm told. Perfect for what I plan to do."

Ella arched a brow. "And what's that?"

The man's face brightened with enthusiasm. "Herbs. I'm an herb farmer. I want to grow everything myself, sell to Amish communities and local stores. The way I see it, people want the natural healing herbs, but not everyone knows where to get organic products."

Ella's breath caught in her throat. "You... you grow herbs?"

"*Jah*," he said, nodding. "Been dreaming of starting my own organic farm for years."

Ella sat up a little straighter. The weight of the bundle in her lap suddenly felt lighter. "That's what I was planning too," she admitted, her voice almost a whisper.

The man's brow lifted in interest. "Really?"

She nodded, tilting the bundle slightly toward him. "My uncle gave me this. It holds our family's best herbal recipes, passed down through generations."

His smile widened. "Sounds like Cashton's about to get two new businesses in one."

Ella chuckled for the first time in weeks, maybe even months... something stirred deep within her.

Hope.

The young man tipped the brim of his straw hat. "I should introduce myself. Joseph Fisher."

Ella hesitated for only a second before smiling and adding, "Ella Stutzman."

Joseph leaned back in his seat, stretching his legs out in front of him. "What do you think is the hardest herb to grow in the Midwest?"

Ella didn't even have to think. "Echinacea. It's stubborn if the soil isn't just right."

He laughed. "That's what I've heard. And the trick to good peppermint?"

She smiled. "Partial shade, lots of water. But you have to keep it from spreading everywhere, or you'll have more peppermint than you know what to do with."

Joseph let out a low whistle. "Sounds like I should take notes."

Ella looked out the window, the rolling landscape blurring past. She hadn't expected this... hadn't expected to sit beside a man who spoke of the same dreams she carried in her heart.

Joseph glanced down at her carefully tied bundle. "If you need a supplier for your shop, I might know a guy."

Ella smirked. "Oh? And what's he charging?"

He chuckled. "The first batch is free. Call it a neighborly gesture."

She laughed, shaking her head. "Generous of you, Joseph Fisher."

He tipped his hat slightly. "I try."

As the bus carried her closer to home, Ella let herself relax. The fear that had chased her for so long was definitely fading, replaced by something new. A future full of possibilities.

Tracy Fredrychowski

event profoundly influenced her, compelling her to dedicate her writing to the peaceful lives of the Amish people. Tracy aims to inspire her readers through her stories to embrace a life centered around faith, family, and community.

For those intrigued by the Amish way of life, Tracy extends an invitation to connect with her on Facebook. On her page and group, she shares captivating Amish photography by her friend Jim Fischer and recipes, short stories, and glimpses into her cherished Amish community nestled deep in the heart of northwestern Pennsylvania's Amish County.

Facebook.com/tracyfredrychowskiauthor/

EPILOGUE

The warm scent of wool filled *Simply Yarn* as Lizzie stepped through the front door. Sunlight streamed in through the windows, catching the neatly arranged skeins of yarn in their bright, cheerful colors. It had been two years since her grandmother's passing, but Esther Yoder's presence still lingered in the small shop, woven into the very fibers of its being.

Miriam looked up from the counter, where she was meticulously sorting through a new shipment. "*Ach*, Lizzie! Just in time. We had another large order come in this morning."

Lizzie smiled as she set down her basket. "You make it sound as if I still run the place."

Miriam chuckled. "It's yours, I'm just keeping it going." She reached over and squeezed Lizzie's hand. "But I'm grateful, *jah*. This shop gives me purpose."

Lizzie's eyes swept across the store, taking in the knitting

circle gathered near the front window, their quiet laughter and rhythmic clicking of needles filling the space with life. The shop had grown in ways her grandmother would have never imagined. They now carried a wider variety of yarns, including specialty fibers from Amish and Mennonite suppliers across the region. And the classes... *oh, how the Englisch women loved their classes!*

"She'd be happy, wouldn't she?" Lizzie murmured, her thoughts drifting back to her grandmother.

Miriam nodded, her expression soft. "*Jah*, she would be proud. The shop, the community, and you, Lizzie. You and Evert built a life that honors everything she stood for."

***

Out behind the shop, the small yard of Esther's cottage had transformed into a thriving garden. Thomas knelt beside a row of carrots, carefully patting the soil down, while Evert leaned on the fence post, watching him with amusement.

"*Datt*, you've outdone yourself," Evert said, shaking his head. "This was supposed to be a flower garden."

Thomas snorted. "Flowers don't feed a family. Vegetables

do." He wiped his hands on his trousers and stood. "Besides, I need something to keep me busy now that Miriam has taken over the shop."

Evert chuckled. "*Jah*, well, don't go planting over the buggy shop too. Isaiah and I need that space."

Thomas gave him a knowing look. "So, it's true then? You two are expanding?"

Evert nodded. "We're adding another workspace so we can handle more than one buggy at a time. Orders keep coming in faster than we can finish them. It's hard to believe how much has changed in two years."

Thomas rested a hand on his son's shoulder. "*Jah*, but change isn't always a bad thing."

They stood in silence for a moment before Thomas spoke again, his voice quieter. "I'm proud of you, Evert. Joining the church, committing to the life you were meant to live… it takes courage to come back."

Evert hesitated before asking the question that had lingered in his mind for some time. "Do you miss it?"

Thomas exhaled, his eyes wandering across the fields. "The Amish way?" He shook his head. "That time has passed for me. I've made peace with who I am. And for the first time in a long

time, I feel accepted here. Willow Springs has been good to us."

Evert absorbed his father's words, finally understanding the depth of his journey. Thomas had found his own path, and in doing so, had made space for Evert to find his.

***

Back inside the shop, Lizzie settled into a rocking chair near the counter, resting her hands over the swell of her belly. "Miriam, do you ever think about slowing down?"

Miriam laughed. "And do what? Sit around waiting for Thomas to bring me vegetables I don't need?"

Lizzie smirked. "You could teach more classes."

Miriam's eyes twinkled. "*Ach*, maybe. But I think you'll be back here soon enough. I know you love this shop."

Lizzie ran her fingers over the arm of the rocking chair, imagining a time when she would return; not as the shopkeeper, but as a mentor, a mother bringing her children to see what their great-grandmother built.

"*Jah*," she admitted. "I'll be back. But for now, I have other dreams to tend to."

Miriam nodded approvingly, and as Evert walked in, his

eyes immediately seeking Lizzie's, she knew her dreams were already coming true.

Speaking of which, Evert nudged her lightly. "Come see what Isaiah and I did at the shop this morning," he said, his tone filled with excitement. "We finished the new buggy stall, and I think we'll be ready to take on more orders in a few weeks."

Lizzie smiled as she took his arm. The man she had once known as a restless soul had found peace here, within the Amish community, within their home, and within himself.

As they strolled toward the buggy shop, Lizzie added, "They're happy."

"They're *home*," Evert corrected, reaching over to squeeze her hand.

Lizzie turned back for just a moment, her gaze drifting to the garden, the shop, the man by her side, everything that had brought them to this place. The threads of her grandmother's life were stitched into every corner of it, into every breath of home that surrounded them now.

In Esther's passing, they had uncovered not just truth, but purpose. In loss, they'd found each other.

Just like every stitch held a story, every choice led them closer to the lives they were meant to live together. And as the

last light of day settled over Willow Springs, Lizzie felt it deep in her heart... this was where healing began, where love grew strong, and where hope, like yarn in practiced hands, was spun into something lasting.

***

Ready for More Mystery in Amish Country?

Welcome to Sweet Briar, a quiet Amish town in Geauga County, Ohio, where secrets run deep and three elderly women have a knack for uncovering the truth.

In the *Amish Book Club Mystery Series*, Rosie, Irma, and Lovina gather each month to discuss their latest mystery novel, only to find themselves drawn into real-life investigations that mirror the pages they read. With the help of Lucy Fisher, a former Amish woman who runs the local diner, and English sheriff Johnathan Carr, this unlikely team of elderly sleuths stirs up more trouble than they solve... or so the sheriff says.

Start the series with...

Buried Secrets: An Amish Book Club Mystery

WHAT DID YOU THINK?

First of all, thank you for purchasing *The Amish Widow's Last Stitch – A Willow Springs Mystery Romance*. I hope you will enjoy all the books in this series.

You could have picked any number of books to read, but you chose this book, and for that, I am incredibly grateful. I hope it added value and quality to your everyday life. If so, it would be nice to share this book with your friends and family on social media.

If you enjoyed this book and found some benefit in reading it, I'd like to hear from you and hope that you would take some time to post a review on Amazon. Your feedback and support will help me improve my writing craft for future projects.

If you loved visiting Willow Springs, I invite you to sign up for my private email list, where you'll get to explore more of the characters of this Amish Community.

Sign up at https://dl.bookfunnel.com/v9wmnj7kve and download the novella that starts this series, *The Amish Women of Lawrence County*.

GLOSSARY
Pennsylvania Dutch "Deutsch" Words

Ausbund. Amish songbook.

bruder. Brother.

denki. Thank You.

doddi. Grandfather.

doddi house. A small house next to the main house.

g'may. Community

goot meiya. Good morning.

jah. Yes.

kapp. Covering or prayer cap.

kinner. Children.

mamm. Mother or mom.

mommi. Grandmother.

nee. No.

Ordnung. Order or set of rules the Amish follow.

rumshpringa. Running around period.

schwester. Sister.

singeon. Singing/youth gathering.

The Amish are a religious group typically referred to as Pennsylvania Dutch, Pennsylvania Germans, or Pennsylvania Deutsch. They are descendants of early German immigrants to Pennsylvania and their beliefs center around living a conservative lifestyle. They arrived between the late 1600s and the early 1800s to escape religious persecutions in Europe. They first settled in Pennsylvania with the promise of religious freedom by William Penn. Most Pennsylvania Dutch still speak a variation of their original German language as well as English.

ABOUT THE AUTHOR

Tracy Fredrychowski's life closely mirrors the gentle, simple stories she crafts in her writing. With a passion for the simple side of life, Tracy regularly shares tips on her website and blog at tracyfredrychowski.com.

In northwestern Pennsylvania, Tracy grew up steeped in the virtues of country living. A pivotal moment in her life was the tragic murder of a young Amish woman in her community. This